A Love Haunting

SUZI ALBRACHT

ISBN-13:978-1983692000
ISBN-10:198369200X

•

DEDICATION

This book is dedicated to Tim who shows me every day
that he is one of the good guys.

CONTENTS

ACKNOWLEDGMENTS

I would like to thank Stephen King and William Faulkner for providing me with endless inspiration. I would also like to thank every teacher I ever had who encouraged me to write. They are my heroes.

CHAPTER 1

Every woman needs a man who will love them to the end of time. A man who puts her needs before his. A man who takes her breath away with a single glance. A man who will do whatever it takes to have a last goodbye kiss.

***

"What do you have there, Baby?" Jordan Snow took his eyes off the road for a brief second to glance at his wife, Emily.

Her oohing sounds had grabbed his curiosity, but Jordan didn't need an excuse to gaze at Emily. From the little bump on the bridge of her nose to her svelte calves, he loved looking at his wife.

"The Christmas ornament I bought today for our new baby. Isn't it beautiful?"

Jordan quickly glanced at the shiny bauble she dangled between them.

"Blue? What if it's a girl?"

Giggling, Emily slipped another ornament from the bag on her lap. "I know, right? I bought two."

Her squeal of delight made him want to stop the car and kiss her.

Is it wrong to love your wife that much?

"Pink and blue. Good thinking, little one," Jordan chuckled.

Emily pushed her blond hair back behind one ear and held the blue bauble in front of her. "Now we'll have a keepsake of our baby's first Christmas. I know someone who can engrave it for us once we pick a name.'"

"And what about the ornament we don't use?"

"Maybe we'll use it for baby number two."

"Baby number two, huh. Then I guess that means we have a plan." Squeezing Emily's hand, he asked, "Did you have a good vacation?"

Emily leaned in, laying her head on her husband's shoulder and wrapping an arm around his. "I had the best time ever. I'm so glad we got to see one last sunset as a couple. The next time we come down for vacation, there will be three of us."

Jordan brought Emily's fingers to his lips and kissed them. His wife was wearing that orchid colored nail polish that reminded him of the silk sheets waiting for them at home.

"It was perfect, wasn't it? You better check your seatbelt. Wouldn't want anything to happen to our little baby."

"Yes sir, Mr. Snow." Emily saluted Jordan. He shook his head, laughing.

"Girl, what am I going to do with you?" Jordan asked, getting a giggle out of his wife.

"Are you excited about starting your internship on Monday? I so can't believe you're finally going to be a surgeon." Emily's voice was excited, pleasing Jordan.

"Let's hope I don't wet my pants my first day," Jordan said, his voice solemn, sparking an eye roll from Emily. "I keep pinching myself because I'm sure I'm dreaming."

Jordan gave a quick glance toward Emily, his grin conveying all the love he had in his heart for her before turning back to concentrate on his driving.

He was determined to get his wife and soon to be newborn home to Annapolis before daybreak. Jordan couldn't wait for the next phase of their lives to begin.

***

Meanwhile...

Six miles away, an old Ford Fairlane station wagon with dirty tinted windows and a plastering of band promotion stickers across the back window, came rumbling out of a side road with tires spitting gravel. The clunker turned onto the highway with a jolt.

Inside, five boys and four girls, all between the ages of fourteen and nineteen, were packed in like sardines, either squeezed against each other or sitting on laps. They had left a kegger a few minutes earlier and were hurrying home to meet their curfews.

Traveling at over 60 miles per hour, the station wagon drifted over the center lane as the driver, Chad Rivers, leaned over to grab the cigarette he dropped on the car's floor. Next to him, his best friend, Rick Anderson, paid no attention to Chad as he rooted around his feet for the lit butt. Instead, Rick twisted in his seat to see what the others were doing in the backseat. Wanting to be the center of attention, he took off his seatbelt and got up on his knees, facing the others.

Rick leaned over the back of his seat and began to belt out the lyrics to the hard rock song on the radio. Soon the others in the backseat joined in. No one was paying attention to the road as they careened into the other lane.

***

Emily saw the station wagon first. She screamed and grabbed onto Jordan's arm, pointing at the station wagon racing toward them in their lane. "Jordan! Look out!"

***

Inside the station wagon, Chad Rivers finally snatched his cigarette from the floor and without looking at the road, turned to laugh at something happening behind him. The clunker was now 100 percent in the wrong lane. No one in the station wagon noticed the shiny red sports car they were about to slam into.

***

"Holy crap," Jordan could see right away it was going to be too late to avoid all contact. He gritted his teeth as he twisted the Camaro's wheel, making a hard left, desperate to avoid a head-on collision.

At the last second, the station wagon clipped the right front bumper of the Camaro, sending it flying off the road. Because the impact was a glancing blow to their fender and the alcohol was still working its way through their bloodstreams, none of the teenagers saw or experienced the hit, but it was enough to send the Camaro rocketing past some trees lining the road and flying down a steep embankment.

Inside the car, as it barreled down the embankment, Jordan and Emily turned toward each other, locking eyes.

It was out of their hands now, and they knew it.

Jordan put one hand out to protect his wife and child. Emily lost the ability to scream. She froze, her eyes wide with panic.

Their bodies slammed back and forth in the Camaro in spite of the seat belts. The cherished Christmas ornaments slammed against the windshield, shattering and sending shards of glass into the air.

Jordan's head banged against the window on the driver's door. Emily's head snapped back, burrowing into her headrest. Grabbing the sides of the headrest, Emily held herself stiff against the seat.

At the bottom of the embankment, the Camaro landed on its nose and flipped over onto its roof, crashing through some weeds until it slid into the ditch wall of the culvert, coming to a crashing halt.

***

After the crash, it was eerily quiet except a clicking noise coming from the Camaro's engine and the sound of the station wagon's broken muffler as it sputtered and drove away.

Out on the highway, Chad finally turned around and steered the car back into the correct lane. Oblivious to the accident, most likely because he was drunk, Chad focused on getting home in one piece.

CHAPTER 2

Sometime after the accident, muddy water from the ditch seeped into the Camaro through the crushed door frames and body of the car. The murky liquid covered the headliner. Shredded blades of grass and shattered pieces of ornaments floated in the silty water streaked with blood and human matter.

Inside the Camaro, the occupants were unconscious and not moving.

After several minutes, Jordan awakened, confused and disoriented. A wave of dread floated over him as scenes from the accident flashed before him. The silence was deafening.

Jordan's eyes scanned his surroundings. He could see he was upside down, still strapped in his seat. He also noticed something else - he had no physical sensations of pain or even discomfort. He knew should feel something since he and Emily had both been tossed around in their seats like a popcorn in a hot pan.

Ignoring his lack of sensation for the moment, he could see that one of his arms hung lifelessly at his side. His other arm was entwined in Emily's seat belt, caught between her and the deployed airbag. His own airbag had not inflated.

Jordan's first semi-rational thought after coming to was that he was going to sue the crap out of somebody over his faulty airbag.

I could have slammed my chest into the steering wheel.

Jordan tried to move his free arm, but his body refused to obey. He tried again and again with no success.

Maybe I'm paralyzed. No! That can't be. I just have to make up my mind to find a way to unbuckle my seat belt. Emily needs my help.

Then, something happened that blew his mind. One minute, he was trying to figure out how to get his seatbelt unbuckled without his hands and the next, he found himself standing outside the car.

Whoa… How did I get out here?

He glanced down at his hands and legs only to see himself floating several inches above the ground. He couldn't see his feet because a pool of mist surrounded them.

Oh crap… What is going on?

Jordan bent over and looked directly at the passenger seat where Emily had been seated. He couldn't see if she was all right because the position of the airbag blocked his view. He figured he would have to go to the other side of the car to get a better look at her.

As Jordan pulled back to go to the other side, his eyes slid back across the driver's seat. He could see a body strapped in the driver's seat, hanging upside down. Jordan's eyes moved up to the head. The entire side of the forehead was crushed, broken shards of bone protruded from the wound. Blood from the gaping wound dripped into the water beneath the body.

Jordan moved to get a closer look at the face.

He flew backward into the weeds, screaming and clawing at his clothes.

Within seconds, Jordan mentally chastised himself to get a grip. He told himself, he was the only one who could provide any kind of help to Emily and himself. Mentally slapping his face, Jordan told himself that he had to buck up and get over there to take another look.

He crept back to the driver's window and forced himself to gaze inside.

No, there was no mistake. The body strapped in that driver's seat was his. And that was his face with eyes half open, eyes of the dead.

Sweet Mary… how can that be me? I had my seatbelt on.

Jordan shoved the idea that he was dead to the back of his mind for the moment and floated to the other side of the car. Emily was facing the door. He could immediately see that she was unconscious. Her eyes were closed, and her nostrils fluttered with each labored breath she took. While there appeared to be some bruising on Emily's face, there was no blood dripping from her head or upper body.

He reached for the door, intending to attend to her wounds, only to see his hand go right through the handle of the door and inside the car.

What the—?

Jordan pulled his hand back and tried again. This time, his arm went clean through the door all the way to his elbow. He took a few steps back and stared, first at his arm and then the car door.

From out of nowhere, a plump vulture swooped down, landing on one of the Camaro's tires, not three feet away. Jordan made a shooing motion and attempted to shout at the bird, except no sound came out of him. The vulture went about its business as if no one was there. Jordan tried again to shoo the bird away. The creature behaved as if it couldn't hear or see him.

I must be dead. No, that can't be. Wouldn't I have gone into that light? Get a grip, man. You stared at your own dead face not five minutes ago.

Jordan fell backward into the weeds. Harsh realities were assailing him, left and right. He didn't want to believe he was dead. He couldn't be dead, the first day of his medical internship was on Monday.

I'm going to be a surgeon saving lives. I can't be dead. Not now.

And Emily… they had celebrated their one year anniversary while on vacation. Who was going to father his child for him?

I'm 26 for goodness sake. I have a full life ahead of me.

He snapped to attention.

The baby!

Jordan rushed back to the car and pushed his head into the Camaro. He could see blood on Emily's legs and on the car seat. As Jordan watched, Emily's breathing worsened. All signs indicated that if he didn't do something very soon, she was going to die. He had to get out on the highway to get help.

As fast as he could, he floated to the top of the embankment. Moving to the side of the highway, he searched for cars or trucks.

Where is everyone? Come on. A car... a truck... a bicycle... a hitchhiker. Somebody's gotta come by here.

But it was late at night and traffic was non-existent at that hour. To complicate matters, even if a car did show up, Jordan didn't know how far he could get with his fog feet. He decided he would stand in the middle of the road and wait to flag down anyone who happened to come by. He just hoped that he wasn't one of those invisible ghosts.

Two hours later, just as Jordan was about to admit defeat and return to Emily's side, a miracle occurred... headlights approached in the distance.

CHAPTER 3

It was late when Doug Nolting and fellow paramedic, Ray Johnson, climbed into their ambulance to take the long ride back to the station. Earlier, they had been dispatched to the scene of a burning house. The report stated that there were several victims at the location.

As it turned out, there was no fire-engulfed home, just a burning outhouse. And the burn victim turned out to be a blowup doll someone had propped up next to the structure. It had been a false alarm.

Doug didn't mind so much, but Ray was ticked because he had gotten yanked out of a sound sleep for nothing.

"Damn kids," Ray complained.

"Come on, Ray. You and I did worse in our youth. As I recall, we locked Petey Williams in the port-a-potty and tipped it over on the door so he couldn't get out. I think we were all of sixteen at the time." Doug rapped his fingers on the steering wheel in time to the tune on the radio.

"Hot damn, I forgot. We were wild 'uns, weren't we?"

"Yup." Doug frowned as he stared up ahead. "Hey, what the hell is that?"

Doug leaned over the steering wheel, squinting.

Is that a man in the middle of the highway? Doug asked himself.

He rubbed his eyes and looked again. The man was still there, standing in the road as the ambulance raced toward him. Or was he? His image faded in and out like a hologram. Doug stared, unsure of what he was seeing.

By this time, Ray saw the man as well.

"You're gonna hit him!" Ray shouted, yanking Doug out of his trance.

Ray grabbed the dash with one hand and held on tight to the strap over his door with the other, preparing for possible impact.

Meanwhile, Doug smashed the brake pedal to the floor. Yanking the steering wheel to the right, the ambulance fishtailed as Doug brought the vehicle to a screeching halt. He had narrowly missed the young man. Later, they would find out he was Jordan Snow, one of the summer people who visited the OBX but for now he was just some crazy guy standing in the middle of the road.

Doug and Ray turned to see the near transparent image of a man standing in a swirl of smoke from the ambulance's tires. His clothing was ripped, tattered and bloodstained. The man seemed agitated and anxious.

As Doug and Ray watched, Jordan floated around to face them, his eyes laser-focused on the ambulance as if he were mentally streaming a message to them.

"Can you see him? I mean really see him?" Ray asked. "Is he real?"

"He has to be real, doesn't he? If not, he's a ghost."

Jordan emphatically pointed to the trees across the road. Doug decided to see what the man wanted from them. He noticed several freshly broken branches lying in the grass to the right of the trees. Like a punch to the head, it came to him. There had been an accident! Doug threw open the ambulance door and jumped out.

"There's a vehicle down in the culvert!" Doug shouted.

Running past Jordan, Doug was taken back for an instant when the young man disappeared right before his eyes, only to reappear farther off the road, in the weeds, as if to lead the way.

By this time, Ray joined Doug, grabbing his arm. "See those skid marks on the road leading to the trees? There's gotta be at least one car. You wait here while I go check it out."

Ray took off toward the trees, with Doug right behind him. At the top of the embankment, Ray dropped to his heels and slid down the muddy hill, breaking his slide with one hand. At the bottom, he slipped into the rakish water and waded off into the darkness.

Doug pounded his way through the tall grasses at the top of the embankment, searching for any victims who may have been thrown from the crash.

"One car. Looks like two occupants. Better call dispatch, we're going to need help on this one," Ray shouted to his partner.

Doug raced back to the ambulance as he radioed in a request for police assistance and the coroner. Jumping in the front seat of the ambulance, he flipped on the emergency lights. Then Doug climbed into the back to grab some medical supplies and a spinal backboard.

He was down at Ray's side with the equipment within minutes.

"Driver's DOA. The passenger's in bad shape. Both are still strapped in by their seatbelts," Ray shouted over his shoulder as he checked Emily's vitals.

Doug made his way over to the driver's side of the car to confirm Ray's evaluation. All the air in his lungs was sucked out when he glimpsed the driver's face. It looked like the young man who had flagged them down. Doug raised his eyes to look over at Ray as he worked on cutting loose the passenger's seat belt.

Right behind Ray, Doug could see the young man's ghost. He was hovering over Ray's shoulder, wringing his hands. Doug could see that the man's lips were moving as if he were mumbling something.

Doug couldn't tear his eyes away from watching the ghost. Meanwhile, Ray finally cut his way through the seatbelt and began to slide Emily out of the car, an inch at a time. Doug thought that the ghost looked relieved. So much so that it looked like the ghost was attempting to help Ray lift Emily from the car.

"Doug! Get over here, I need help. Where's that damn backboard?" Ray shouted. Doug ran around to Ray's side and grabbed the backboard lying on the grass near him. Doug slid it under Emily as Ray held her upper body.

By the time Doug glanced again at where the young man's ghost had been standing, he had vanished.

CHAPTER 4

In the Hospital...

Nurse Carol Adkins stepped into the hospital room. Her new nursing assistant, Allie Nolting, accompanied her. A perky girl, cute in a wholesome way some young people have, Allie was scheduled to graduate from nursing school in a few months. She planned to eventually go on to be a nurse practitioner. Today was her first day on the floor.

"This patient is Emily Snow," Nurse Adkins said as she checked the patient's vitals. "A car accident brought her to us a month ago. Her L4 and L5 both suffered burst fractures. She also received a concussion. She's being treated for both conditions with medications and bedrest, and the goal is to stabilize her so her parents can take her back home to Annapolis for continued therapy and medical assistance in a month or so."

Allie gazed at Emily's face. She had long ash blond hair, lush dark eyelashes, and pale skin. She looked a little like Sleeping Beauty to Allie.

"She sleeps a lot?" Allie asked.

"Her medications for pain and infection as well as a muscle relaxant knock her out," Nurse Adkins said as she bushed Emily's hair from her face. "She never complains, even though the pain has to be off the scale."

Allie watched Nurse Adkins fluff Emily's pillow and adjust her sheets and blankets. Looking around the room, Allie noticed every flat surface in the room was covered with flowers, balloons, and stuffed animals.

"It looks like she has plenty of people who love her," Allie said.

"Both parents were here 24/7 for the first month. However, her father's a Senator, so they had to get back to Maryland. Now they come for a visit every Thursday and stay until Monday night." Nurse Adkins gestured toward the stuffed animals. "When they come, they bring these and candy for the staff. Nice people. Her father is extremely popular in the Senate. The President even took the time to call one day."

"I see she's wearing a wedding ring. What about her husband?" Allie asked.

Nurse Adkins glanced at their patient as she whimpered in her sleep. She quickly ushered Allie toward the door.

"Emily lost her husband in the accident and her unborn child. She was due in December."

"Oh, I'm sorry, I didn't mean to..."

Nurse Adkins leaned closer. "It's not your fault, Allie. I should have filled you in before we came into her room."

"I knew about the accident," Allie murmured.

"From the papers?"

"My daddy was one of the paramedics at the scene."

Nurse Adkins stared at Allie's face for a moment. "Strange you didn't mention it earlier."

Allie pushed her hair back behind her ear and said, "I didn't tell anyone because I was afraid of being accused of seeking out the job because I was curious about the patient." Allie looked over at Emily's bed. "You won't fire me, will you?"

"Why would I fire you? I was surprised, nothing more. I'd like to hear about the accident if you don't mind. Later, when we are done with rounds." Nurse Adkins put her hand on Allie's upper arm in a reassuring gesture.

"Sure."

Allie glanced back into the room.

"Hey, who's the guy sitting in the corner?" Allie asked.

"Who?" Nurse Adkins turned to look. "There's nobody there."

Allie glanced again. This time when she looked, she saw that the young man seemed to be around 26 or 27. He was dressed in a blood-stained shirt and jeans. In spite of the bloody, tattered clothing, he was a good-looking guy, tall, muscular physique, longish light brown hair, intensely blue eyes. His attention was focused on Emily.

Allie's gut told her the man had to be Jordan. She also recognized that Nurse Adkins couldn't see him, most likely because she didn't believe in ghosts. Or there was a chance that he didn't want her to see him.

"My mistake, the shadows played tricks on my eyes."

Nurse Adkins looked at her watch. "I'm going to finish our rounds. You can stay and read to Emily. Reading seems to be soothing to her."

After Nurse Adkins left, Allie shut the door. As she walked to the bed, she and Jordan locked eyes. They acknowledged one another with a slight nod. Allie selected a book from the table next to Emily's bed and pulled up a chair. She began to read a love story to Emily. It was easy to see that Emily was happy because her lips curled into a smile.

Meanwhile, Jordan glided over and stretched out on the side of the bed, spooning against Emily and stroking her hair. Allie didn't mind. She loved a good love story.

CHAPTER 5

One Month Later...

Once Emily's medications were cut back, she became more alert. Before long, she and Allie bonded. Right from the start, it seemed they were more like sisters than friends. So it wasn't surprising to anyone when Allie began to spend many of her days off visiting with Emily.

Today, Allie offered to drop by to give Emily a break from the closing walls of her room. She came in earlier that morning to help dress Emily and get her ready for a few hours of fresh air out on the hospital patio. Then Allie assisted Emily into the wheelchair and took her to the outside patio. Parking Emily under a large umbrella, Allie put the brake on so Emily wouldn't roll away.

"Here we are. I have three books for you to choose from today," Allie said as she fanned the paperbacks out in front of Emily. "I suggest the supernatural horror but any of them are good."

As Emily gazed off into the distance, Allie took a quick glance around. She didn't see Jordan anywhere. Whenever Jordan was present, Emily seemed to be more subject to mood changes.

"I feel like Jordy comes to visit me. I know that can't be. Or maybe it can," Emily whispered. "Am I going crazy?"

Allie sat in a chair next to Emily and took her hand.

"I have something to tell you. I'm a sensitive."

"Sensitive? Do you mean you're psychic?" Emily asked.

"Yes. Sometimes, folks call people like me mediums. What that means is that I can see people who have passed, and sometimes, I can communicate with them. Every now and then I can predict future events. And no, I can't predict the lottery."

"And you can see Jordy?"

"I do. Jordan's image is not solid by any means, but it's clear enough to make out his features and expressions," Allie said as she squeezed Emily's hand to reassure her. "He comes to see you every night and almost every day."

"So I'm not crazy... But why can you see him and I can't?" Emily asked.

"Sometimes a person who has passed will appear to some people and not others. It could very well be that Jordan hasn't learned how to show himself to you yet," Allie said.

"Ohhhhh…. What does he look like? Pretty blue eyes? Light brown hair… hangs kinda longish? Tall?" Emily asked, her excitement barely contained.

"That's him."

"Does Jordy look happy?" Emily squeezed Allie's hand. "Tell me everything."

"I've seen him stroke your hair many times. When he does, he almost glows. My granny used to say that was a sign of true love."

Emily leaned back. Her brow crinkled as an idea popped into her head.

"I have to see him. Will you help me? Please?"

"Sweetie, it's not that easy. When someone is newly deceased, they are afraid and fearful of their surroundings. They don't know what to make of their new world. When they don't pass over into Heaven, they have to exist on a different plane. Some never learn how to show themselves." Allie tried to be gentle. Disappointment turned down the corners of Emily's mouth anyway.

"I wish I could see Jordy again. And touch him… And smell him…"

Allie touched Emily's cheek. "He always kisses you, right here before he leaves like he's kissing you goodnight."

"He does?" Emily asked, pulling back.

"Yes. It's sweet… the way he is so gentle with you."

As Emily's eyes welled with tears, she swiped at them with the back of her hand and shook her head as if to put any others back where they came from.

"I'm such a big baby. Don't mind my tears," Emily said. "We have to figure out a way for us to… I don't know… at least see each other."

"You know what? I'd like to know more about you as a couple… before the accident. Would you share some stories with me? I'd love to hear more about Jordan when he was alive."

"Oh, we were such a boring couple," Emily murmured.

"I'll bet you have lots of stories to tell."

Suddenly, Emily's face became animated. Her eyes sparkled, and she wore a smile that would make grumpy old men feel like young boys again.

"I know, I'll share some stories with you from our last vacation. It was our best vacation."

And so she did. Allie thought Emily's voice sounded serene and happy when she spoke, almost like a lover whispering sweet words of forever.

CHAPTER 6

Two Days Before the Accident
Emily's Memories...

"Jordan Alston Snow, I'm going to kill you," I muttered, squirming in my beach chair as I tried to dodge the water my husband was pouring over my head.

A few minutes earlier, I had been leaning back, catching a quick snooze, not hurting a soul. My world was peaceful and tranquil until I was startled out of my doze by a bucket of sea water splashing over my head. Most of the water narrowly missed the book I had dropped on my lap when I dozed off.

Well, I wasn't about to let my husband get away with giving me a dousing. I jumped to my feet, grabbed the bucket and chased Jordan across the beach and into the surf. When I caught him, I dumped bucket after bucket of water over Jordan's head until we both collapsed into the waves, laughing our heads off.

"Are you finished?" Jordan asked.

"For now."

"Good," my hunky hubby said as he grabbed my face and gave me kiss after kiss until I stopped laughing and kissed him back. As if we were choreographed, simultaneously, we fell back onto our rear ends and let the ocean waves splash us.

"Promise me when we retire, we'll move here," Jordan begged in his sexy boy toy voice.

"You don't have to ask me twice. I wish we weren't going home tomorrow. One or two more days would have been nice." I slipped a sideways glance at my husband.

I knew it was wishful thinking. But every year I had the same wish. No matter how great our vacation was, I wanted one more day.

Jordan was silent for a moment. I was hopeful that he was calculating ways to make an extra day work into our schedule. "Tell you what, if you can find us a room, we'll stay one more day," he said, turning to look at me.

I shrieked and climbed onto Jordan's lap, kissing him passionately, almost knocking him over.

"Hey, this is a family beach. You want to get us kicked off?" Jordan hugged me.

"Oooh, the baby just moved." I giggled and put my hand on my baby bump. "Want to feel it?"

Jordan put his hand on my tummy. "Where?"

"No, here," I said as I moved his hand to the exact location.

Jordan's eyes became as big as saucers as our baby kicked. He jumped to his feet and ran around in the surf yelling, "My son just moved. I felt him!"

For a second, the beachgoers around us stared at Jordan, not knowing what to make of his outburst. Then a woman standing nearby noticed my small belly swelling and clapped her hands. Soon others joined in.

"Congrats," the woman said.

Jordan pounded his chest like Tarzan and jumped around in the waves. He looked so cute. I couldn't help myself, I laughed. I was so pleased something so simple could make my husband so happy.

Eventually, Jordan sprinted back to me and held out his hand to help me stand. Then, sweeping me up in his arms, my husband carried me back to shore, all the way to our canopy. There, he had to put me back on my feet while he brushed away the mess he had made.

"Some crazy guy got sand all over your chair." Jordan slipped me that naughty boy grin.

Oh God, I'm in heaven. My heart swelled.

After he wiped away all the sand and salt water, Jordan helped me into my chair as if I were already nine months gone.

My hero. How did I ever get this lucky?

"Want some lunch?"

"I didn't pack anything except snacks," I said.

"I'm thinking something a little more substantial. Remember you are eating for two now, Mrs. Snow. I'm going to drive to Owen's and get something to go."

"Yum. Sounds good. Burger and fries?"

"You got it," Jordan said as he grabbed a tee-shirt and slipped it on. Snatching his keys with one hand and his sandals with the other, he headed for the main road.

"Hey, Jordy?" I called out.

"Yes, Baby?"

"Pie. I want a slice of coconut pie, too." I giggled. Ever since I got pregnant, I couldn't seem to get enough of pie… and cupcakes. Especially coconut ones.

"Coconut? What if they don't have coconut?"

I burst into tears. And there was the second habit I had acquired in my pregnancy. I'll be the first to admit that I've always been a crier, however, now I was a serial crier. I cried over everything. You name it, I cried. Shoot, once I cried because the mailman was singing when he brought the mail to our box.

My tears never lasted long, but poor Jordy never knew how to handle them or me when they popped up out of nowhere. Whenever I cried, I think he felt like a bull in a china shop, everywhere he turned, he broke something. There was nowhere he could turn and not do damage of some sort. I know my crying worried him. That was the problem with him being a doctor, he was always looking for a cure. And trust me, there is no cure for baby blues.

Anyway, a couple of dabs at my eyes with my beach towel and my crying jag was over. But Jordan took a few steps toward me. I'm sure he wanted to ensure I was all right so I put my hand up to stop him.

"It's the hormones, sweetie. Just the hormones. Cherry pie will do."

Jordan shook his head, "Nope, my Baby wants coconut so I will scour the entire OBX until I find a slice."

Turning, Jordan continued to the beach access way.

The woman under the beach canopy next to ours caught my eye and said, "You've got a good man there."

I beamed. "The best."

CHAPTER 7

One Night Before the Accident...

After spending the day at the beach, we had our traditional next-to-last night-dinner at Mama Kwan's. That dinner was always a melancholy event. Tonight was no different. Jordan and I held hands while we ate.

"Jordy?" I asked.

"Yes, Baby?"

God... his voice makes my heart sing. I hope this feeling never ends.

"Do you think your parents would approve of us?" I asked.

Our coming baby had got me thinking about the Ragans. They had always been a touchy subject we both avoided. The Ragans were Jordy's birth parents. And no, he hadn't been taken away from them, nor had they given him up for adoption. They had been murdered one hot August night by an angry neighbor.

Poor Jordan had been the sole survivor. He had been barely five when it happened, and it had taken him years to trust people again. By the time I met Jordan, he had been adopted by the Snows, a lovely couple in our church.

"I remember enough of them to know they would have loved you. I have a photo in my wallet," Jordan said in a quiet voice.

"Jordan Snow, you never told me you had a photo. Let me see it, please."

My husband slipped his wallet from his pocket and pulled out a worn photo. It had been laminated to keep the edges from fraying. He placed the picture on the table in front of me. As I looked at it, a great sorrow squeezed my heart. While Jordan had his mother's coloring, he was the spitting image of his father.

Instantly, my heart broke for him. Hot tears flowed down my cheeks and splashed onto my fish tacos.

Jordan wiped away my tears with his napkin. "Someday, when we have lived our lives, they will meet us and lead us into Heaven."

I was so surprised to hear Jordan speak of Heaven and the afterlife. I raised my eyes to gaze at him. "You're not angry at them anymore?"

"No, that was the child in me. Now I've matured and had a change of heart. I would have told you before but… I don't know. It just never seemed like the right time to bring it up. I did a lot of soul-searching while I was volunteering at the church that made me see things differently. I don't want to bring anger to my own child."

"I am glad, Jordy. I hated what the memories of that night were doing to you."

"I understand now that it wasn't their fault that their friend would end up murdering them. And I know my mother saved my life when she hid me in that closet with my puppy while my father fought with their murderer." Jordan stared at the photo. He touched the images with a fingertip and let a tiny smile slip onto his lips.

"They must have loved you so much." I rubbed the knuckles on the hand he had clenched in his lap.

"The last thing my mother said was for me to remember that she and daddy loved me. At the time, I was so scared and could only think about how Mr. Davis was going to hurt my puppy too. Now, I wonder if I could have saved them. Maybe I could have run for the phone and called the police."

"You were too little. There was nothing you could have done." I stared into Jordan's eyes to convince him. I hoped I succeeded, if only a little bit.

"Anyway, I know they would have loved you." Jordan sighed and began biting his lower lip. It was something he did when he was thinking about something.

"Thank God for the Snow family."

"I don't know what would have happened if they hadn't taken me in.

"Mommy always said you got a Christmas miracle."

"And now I'm about to get another Christmas miracle. I'm going to be a father." Jordan's eyes widened. "I'm going to be a father. Wow."

"You're going to be a great dad. Jordy. Ummmmm…. before we go home, I want to buy a keepsake for the baby. A memory of his almost first vacation at the beach."

"You know it could be a girl, don't you? I mean girls do run in your family." Jordan reminded me.

"So do twins. Wild, right? Maybe we'll have one of each."

We grinned at each other for a few seconds before we began to eat our dinner again and hold hands. The photo was still on the table between us, and I'll admit it, I couldn't take my eyes off of it. For some reason, it drew me in. I hoped Jordan, and I would have many more years together than his poor parents had gotten.

"After dinner, let's grab some cones from the Kill Devil's Grill," Jordan said. "I thought tomorrow we could have one last beach day. And then, if you are a good girl, we'll do a little shopping in Duck just before we head home. We'll look for a keepsake trinket and maybe a few cute tops for you. I saw some the other day that would look great on you."

"Good girl? I don't know if I can be any better," I teased.

Jordan tickled my hand until I gave in.

"Okay, okay. I'll be a good girl," I smirked.

"Want to see a movie tonight?" Jordan put his arm around me.

"I am so spoiled." I leaned into my husband's chest. I could feel his heart beating. As I reached to stroke his cheek, I looked over to see a small boy at the next table watching us.

"Ewww, Momma. They're going to kiss again," The boy complained to his mother, and buried his head in her shirt.

The mother, to her credit, comforted her son and smiled at us over his head. I don't know about Jordan, but it was all I could do not to laugh. That boy was so cute.

"No more kissing," I chastised Jordan.

"Yes, ma'am," Jordan replied as he leaned in and stole a quick kiss from me.

The boy peeked and squealed, "Mommmmmm, they're doing it again."

Jordan and I lost it, we couldn't keep a straight face. Everyone in our section of the restaurant laughed until we couldn't anymore. This was going to be one of my fondest memories.

CHAPTER 8

The Morning of the Accident...

"Wakie wakie, sleepy head," My way-too-happy-in-the-morning husband called from the bathroom.

Geez, didn't the man ever sleep?

I growled, well okay, I thought about growling. Who can be irritated in paradise?

"I'm awake." I glanced at the clock on the nightstand. Eleven o'clock. It must have driven him crazy to let me sleep so late.

With a sigh, I swung my legs over the side of the bed and stretched. I was already feeling a little bluesy. Today was going home day and as I did every year, I hated it. And then it hit me.

"You better get done in there real quick. Mommy's got morning sickness and —" I jumped to my feet and sprinted on my tiptoes to the bathroom. I barely made it.

A second later, I was on my knees gripping the sides of the commode as hard as I could with my face staring at the commode's porcelain walls. Jordy stood behind me, holding my hair out of harm's way.

"Hey... Babe... I think you can let go. It can't go anywhere."

I started to flip him the finger, stopping only because I remembered our pact. We had made an agreement that we were going to act like adults until our child went to college. Jordy and I had a bet going to see who would break first. I was determined that I was going to win but it was hard. Old habits die hard, you know? The prize was a month of pampering and right about now I needed that so I was going do my darndest to win.

Take that, Jordy!

Anyway, I pulled back onto my haunches. I felt like my morning sickness had passed, so I told myself to get going. I still had some packing to do before we headed out for the day. Sighing, I started to get up on my feet. Halfway up, I bent over, barfing on Jordy's feet.

And do you know what my big lug of a husband did? He calmly took some Kleenex and wiped his feet and the floor, dumping the used tissues in the toilet. When that was done, he walked over to the shower and turned it on. And while the shower water was heating up, he grabbed the disinfectant from the back of the commode, sprayed the affected area and wiped away the mess. Lastly, he leaned me against the wall, stripped us both and ushered me into the shower.

It was the best late morning I had all vacation. We lathered each other to our hearts' content, and when we got clean, we got dirty all over again.

And again.

Like I said, it was the best late morning ever.

CHAPTER 9

The Night of the Accident...

After an afternoon of shopping, we drove the Camaro over to the Black Pelican for a nice dinner before heading home.

When the hostess offered to seat us, I requested a table near the front hostess desk. She led us over to a table and gave us menus to look at. Jordan opened his menu and then shut it. The man never tried anything new. I went back and forth between a couple of dishes, trying to make a decision. But my mind kept wandering. I was thinking about the ghosts of The Black Pelican.

Some time ago, I had developed a bit of curiosity about the tale of T.L. Daniels who had been killed at Station Six, a lifesaving station at the time. The Station Six building no longer exists. However, when The Black Pelican was built on the site, it retained a part of Station Six.

According to lore, in the 1800s, Captain James Hobbs was the keeper of Station Six. It was said that Daniels wanted Hobbs' job, so he turned Hobbs into the authorities for using government paint from the station on his own personal boat. As a result, a meeting was set up with Lt. E.C. Clayton, Hobbs' superior, which somehow turned into a gun battle between Hobbs and Daniels.

Some pieces of the story seemed unclear, but one fact was always the same – Daniels was the only person who ended up dead that day. And Daniels is said to haunt The Black Pelican to this day.

The story fascinated me so much that I always asked to sit near the supposed spot where Daniels fell dead, by the hostess stand. I know how morbid it sounds, but it wasn't like he died last month or anything.

Anyway, I had my mind set on finding out more about the hauntings at The Black Pelican. Besides T.L. Daniels, I was also interested in exploring some other ghost stories about several ladies whose husbands went to sea but never returned. Some claim the ladies also remain stuck at The Pelican, waiting forever. I've never seen anything, but I had hopes of seeing a ghost one day. And so I always sat near the hostess stand, keeping my eye out for Daniels and the ladies.

***

An Hour Later…

I chanced a glance inside my purse when I thought Jordy wasn't looking.

"What are you doing?" Jordan finger-shamed me.

"Nothing."

Geez, I had to go and marry a guy who noticed all the little things, didn't I?

Jordan grabbed my hand from my purse.

Darn, he was so nosey.

Jordan didn't know I was so itching to get contact with one of the ghosts of The Pelican that I came prepared… just in case. I had gotten that itch a few months back when I looked into ghost hunting. Others had some remarkable success stories of contacting ghosts, I wanted my chance too.

To get prepared, I watched several ghost hunter shows on television to get some tips. In every episode, I noticed that they used the same types of cameras, recorders, and meters. I liked the idea of a ghost meter so I bought one on Amazon and was dying to see if the red lights would blink for me. Knowing we were going to The Pelican for dinner, I had slipped my meter into my purse ahead of time.

I had thought maybe I could do my sleuthing without Jordan being any the wiser. I should have known better. We had been together a long time and never kept secrets from each other. It was too late to start now.

And now Jordan leaned over and looked inside my purse. Grinning he said, "At least put it where I can see it too."

My husband is the best.

"There aren't many people here tonight. Maybe we'll get lucky and a ghost will talk to us," I suggested.

Jordan began to cram his blackberry pie into his mouth. Even though I had my own piece of coconut pie, I stole a forkful of his. Laughing, he moved his plate out of my reach.

I started to protest when Jordan got a funny look on his face like he had stepped on something squishy. He squeezed his shoulders together and said, "Ooooh... I got a chill just now."

The red lights on the ghost meter lit up like it was Christmas. Jordan touched it with a finger, and the red flashes came faster. We turned to stare at each other.

"Ask it something," Jordan whispered.

"Are you a man?"

Speak to me T.L., make the lights blink.

The lights went crazy.

OMG, is he responding to my request?

I glanced around and saw we were alone in the dining room except for our waitress who was reading a book in the far corner.

"Good. Did you die in the last 50 years?" I asked, raising my eyebrows at Jordan.

The lights stayed silent, not one flicker.

"Did you pass more than 50 years ago?"

Again, not one flicker. I was about to stick the thing back in my purse when the lights went nuts again. I asked the question I had been carrying around ever since I had purchased the ghost meter.

"Are you T.L. Daniels?"

The red lights flashed once, stopped a few moments, and flashed again before going dark.

"It's him!" Jordan grabbed my hand and squeezed in excitement. "Ask him if anyone else is with him."

"Mr. Daniels, we appreciate your response. Is there anyone with you?"

The lights flashed twice.

"Two? Does that mean two people are with you?"

Two flashes were my answer.

"Okay. Two men?"

Nothing.

"Two children?"

Nothing.

"Two women?"

The lights went nuts.

"Woo hoo. I can't believe it. T.L. Daniels, Baby. Who do you think the two women are?" Jordy asked.

"I read stories about when this used to be the Kitty Hawk Life-Saving Station. Sometimes when the wives and mothers of sailors got word that their ships were in danger, they came to the Station to wait for word and pray for their loved ones. Some of those husbands and sons never came home and were lost at sea. Grief could make their ghosts stick around," I said.

"And I read that they nicknamed this area the Graveyard of the Atlantic," Jordan said. Rather proudly to my shock.

Wow. All this time, I thought my husband didn't believe in ghosts.

"And here I was under the impression that you spent all your internet research on medical information," I teased.

"Hey, I'm a master of a lot of things. I know about the Cora tree too. We should check it out on our next vacation here."

I looked at him and shook my head in amazement.

Wow. Wow. Wow.

I leaned over the meter and spoke softly.

"Two women?"

The lights lit up even redder than before. They stayed red for a full minute. About twenty seconds in, Jordan stood up and walked to the window to look outside. When he came back, Jordy put his hands on the back of his chair and leaned in toward me. He mouthed, 'this can't be real.'

The lights stopped.

"Are the women friends of yours?

Nothing.

"Are they family members?"

Nothing. In fact, after our initial exchange, we couldn't get a single response out of the meter. No matter what we asked, the lights remained dark. Jordan and I were both deflated and excited at the same time.

"Jordy… wow…"

"I know… right? We have to try again," Jordan said as he examined the meter.

"Next year we have to bring a spirit box," I said, thinking ahead.

"Next year?" Jordan looked at me confused at first, and then it came to him. "Right, we're going home tonight," he said, glancing at his watch. "Speaking of which, we better get going, or it will be tomorrow morning by the time we get home. Ready?"

As my husband summoned our waitress, a strange sensation washed over me as if someone were watching us. No, it was more like they had their sights set on Jordan. I glanced around the room. I swear I caught a glimpse of an angry man in a seafarer's cap in a reflection off a window across the room.

"Ready, sweetie?" Jordan touched my hand.

"What? Oh… yes. We better get on the road."

"If you're not feeling well, we could get a room for the night."

"No, I'm tired of sleeping in other people's beds," I said, gathering my things.

Jordan laughed and put his arm around my shoulders. If only I had known what was waiting for us on the road home.

CHAPTER 10

Back to Present Day...

"See? I told you we were boring."

"No way. I loved hearing about your vacation, and I want to hear more. But I can see you're tired. Besides, we should get you inside. Tomorrow's a big day for you." Allie said as she stood and released the brake on Emily's wheelchair. She pushed the chair toward the hospital entrance.

"I wish you'd reconsider," Emily murmured.

"I wish I could, but I have to finish school. Besides, you need me to get things ready for when you return. You won't change your mind and decide to stay in Annapolis, will you?"

Allie glanced at her side. Jordan was walking next to her. His image was flickering in and out of focus. He made eye contact with Allie as if he was trying to give her a message. She frowned. She wondered if she should say something to Emily.

"Not a chance. I love my family but my heart is here. It always has been. Daddy and Mommy want me in Maryland so they can watch over me. Daddy even offered to buy me a summer place here. But they know that ultimately it's my choice."

As they kept moving, Jordan floated in front of them. He did it so rapidly Allie didn't have time to stop. She plowed through his image, stopping mere inches past him.

"Is something wrong, Allie?"

"Jordan is here."

Emily grabbed the wheels on her wheelchair and whipped around to face Allie.

"Where?" She asked, staring at Allie.

Allie pointed to a spot next to the wheelchair.

Emily stared at the spot.

"I can't see him."

At this point, Jordan was flickering in and out like a firefly being drained of his juice.

"He's having trouble. Maybe it's too bright out here."

Jordan bobbed his head in response.

"Yes... the light's a problem. Let's go to your room."

"Hurry. I don't want Jordan to leave," Emily said.

Allie pushed Emily's wheelchair as quickly as she could to the entrance.

***

The moment they entered Emily's room, Allie shut the door. Jordan was already there. He was standing by the window as if to tell Allie to close the drapes. So she did.

Once Allie got the drapes shut, she watched Jordan float over and do a floating kneel at Emily's feet.

"Em? He's right in front of you… at your feet."

"I don't see him," Emily cried out.

"Hold your hand out. Do you feel a cold spot?"

Emily reached out several inches before she found the right spot. Allie could see that Emily's hand was touching Jordan's face at the top of his right cheek.

"Is it? I mean, is that Jordy?"

"It is."

"Oh… Jordy…"

Jordan put his fingers out to touch Emily. Allie could see the frustration on his face. She opened her mouth to reassure him, but he disappeared. Just like that. Poof. Gone.

The instant that happened, Emily pulled back, fighting back the tears. "He's gone, isn't he?" Emily asked.

Allie didn't want to confirm Emily's fear. She began to fiddle with her hair.

"He'll be back… he'll be back when he can. I know that now so I can wait," Emily whispered.

"I have the feeling that when he does, he's going to surprise you," Allie said.

Out of the corner of her eye, Allie noticed Jordan standing outside the room. He was watching Emily through the window on the door. Allie watched him fade into nothing.

CHAPTER 11

It was after midnight when Allie finally left the hospital. She was exhausted and still had to be back early in the morning to get Emily ready for her trip to Maryland.

The parking garage elevator doors opened on the fifth level, and Allie stepped out. The single thing she had on her mind was the soft down comforter she was planning to wrap herself in once she got home. She quickened her step, and within seconds, around the bend, her car came into view.

The parking garage was almost empty. When Allie arrived at her car, it was the only car on that level. She was thankful for the bright garage lights. Using her clicker to open her car door, Allie slid inside. After adjusting the rear view mirror, she reached over to snap her seat belt.

"Hi."

Allie stopped cold.

Who said that?

Allie twisted in her seat, looking to see where the sound had come from. However, there was nothing and no one to be seen. She rolled down her window and listened for a few seconds, but she didn't hear the voice again. She told herself that her imagination was working overtime.

Turning back around, she almost jumped out of her skin because sitting in her passenger seat was none other than Jordan Snow.

"Oh my God. Jordan, I almost wet my pants."

Jordan grinned.

"Did you say hi?"

Jordan nodded.

"Can you try it again?"

The first time Jordan tried, nothing came out, not even the sound of air. Allie put her hand up to stop him.

"My granny said when ghosts want to talk, they have to concentrate all their energy to form a sound. Try pulling strength from your toes all the way to the top of your head."

Jordan concentrated and tried again. This time his 'hi' exploded from his mouth. Allie's hands flew to cover her ears, her hair blew back from the force of his speech. Blood dripped from her nose. She grabbed a Kleenex from the console and dabbed at the blood.

"Ummm…. better but it's a little loud. Do the same thing you just did, only this time, let your words form naturally and not be forced out."

Jordan reached out his hand as if he was trying to touch her face. She flinched, but his words reassured her.

"I… won't… hurt… you. Want… to make sure… didn't burst… a vein in your nose."

Jordan leaned in to visually examine her nose as a doctor would do. *Just as he had done probably more than once when he was alive and treating patients*, Allie mused.

When it occurred to her that Jordan had actually spoken, she smiled at him.

"Jordan…"

"You heard me," Jordan said, his face shiny with amazement.

Allie touched her nose and squinted from the pain. "Your voice sounds like an old out of tune radio, but I can make out what you are saying."

"Well, thanks for the compliment," Jordan laughed. When Allie looked embarrassed, he said, "I'm teasing."

While he was able to speak full sentences now, Allie didn't like the way Jordan's image flickered in and out.

"You should take it easy on speaking, you're using too much energy," Allie warned. "Did you come to see me because you wanted something? Nod or shake your head."

Jordan nodded.

"Is it about Emily?"

Another nod.

Suddenly a light flooded the interior of the car. Allie turned to look. A security guard stood by her window, flashlight in hand.

"Ma'am? Is everything okay?"

Allie lowered her window and looked up at the officer.

"I'm fine. Just listening to the radio."

"You shouldn't be hanging around in the garage this late at night," the guard chastised.

"You're right. I'll be heading home now. Thank you." Allie turned her car key in the ignition.

"You drive safe now. Your gentleman friend, too."

Allie turned to look at Jordan. The look of surprise on his face was comical. His mouth was wide open, and his eyebrows were up in the air like birds flying. She giggled.

"Have a great night, officer," Allie said as she turned on her car and rolled up the window. "Relax, Jordan. I'll drive down the street and park in the Denny's parking lot."

The officer took a few steps back to let her pull out of her parking space. Allie waived at him and drove off.

***

"I can't believe the guard saw you," Allie exclaimed. "You know he thought we were making out, right?"

Jordan's grin almost glowed.

"I know you came to me because you need something. You want me to tell Emily something, right?"

"Yes... I want her to work on getting healthy again... I want her... I want her to live a full life. If that means she has to put me in the past, then that is what she has to do." Jordan hung his head, his shoulders slumped. Allie's heart broke for him.

"I know you want the best for her, Jordan. And I know it hurts for you to admit she needs to live a good life without you. Emily told me what a good man you are. I can see she's right."

"Tell her I love her, and that I'll come to see her when I can. I won't intrude on her life. Tell her — "

And with that, Jordan disappeared. Allie waited a few minutes in case he was able to come back but the wait was for nothing. After waiting twenty minutes, she drove home.

CHAPTER 12

The next morning, the private ambulance was already at the hospital when Allie got there. Shortly after, Emily's parents arrived in a chauffeured town car. The plan was for Emily's mother to ride in the ambulance with Emily, and her father would follow behind in the car.

Allie had packed all of Emily's things the night before, so she was ready to go. Once the paperwork was done, the ambulance drivers rolled Emily out of the hospital on a stretcher. Allie walked alongside her carrying a bag full of stuffed animals and holding her hand.

Emily handed Allie a sheet of paper she had been clutching. "Here's my email and cell phone numbers. I still wish you'd ride up with us."

Allie chanced a quick look at Emily. Her body was so small and frail on the gurney. And her eyes pleaded with Allie. Even though she hated to say no, Allie had no choice.

"You know I heard the hospital where you'll be staying has some super cute doctors. I'd be too distracted to be of much help to you."

Emily laughed. "True. You're right, I can't trust you around a cute doctor." Her face got serious as Emily said, "Allie, you were the first friend I made after…" Her voice faded as she looked off into the distance.

"I'll be here when you get back."

Emily glanced over at her parents. They were busy talking to her doctors and the ambulance drivers. Her father was towering over one of the drivers. Emily knew her father well enough to know he was lecturing the driver and the other paramedic about avoiding bumps in the road and keeping the radio low. She also knew her mother was going right behind him and bribing them with event tickets and dinner passes. Emily always thought her parents were made for each other, times like this confirmed it.

"Will Jordan follow me?"

"He'll want to, but if Jordan does come, he won't be able to stay long. It takes a long time for a ghost to gather strength to travel or project his image."

"Maybe I should stay. I can do my therapy here." Emily's eyes pleaded with her again. Allie knew Emily wanted her to agree but she couldn't. It wouldn't be fair to Emily.

"No, Jordan wouldn't want you to stay here when you can get more advanced therapy at George Washington University Hospital. You won't find specialists like those D.C. doctors around here unless they are on vacation. Get your surgery and therapy. Jordan's not going anywhere. Whether you stay there a year or twenty, it will seem like a minute to him."

"But—"

"Jordan specifically asked for you to have a good life. You don't want to disappoint him, do you?"

"No."

Emily covered her eyes with her hands. Allie gently pushed Emily's hands down and looked into her eyes.

"Please go to Maryland and do what you have to do to get healthy. Jordan and I will be waiting for you to come back."

"I need a hug," Emily whispered.

Allie leaned over and obliged as best she could without hurting her friend.

"I'm glad I met you. I only wish it had been on the beach and not in a hospital room," Emily said.

"Me, too." Allie glanced over at Emily's parents. "It looks like your dad's about to go off on the driver. Is he always so intense?"

"Yes. Daddy has strict rules about how to treat his women. Mom and I know he's a softie inside. He can be fierce with others. I heard whispers that in D.C. he is feared."

"No kidding."

Emily watched Allie for a few minutes, contemplating what to say next.

"I've been thinking about when I come back. First I'll get settled, and you will move in with me. And then when we're ready, I want to visit all my old haunts. Mama Kwan's, Kelly's, The Flying Fish, oh, and that restaurant in Duck that reminds me of Key West. I'll go to every place I can until I find Jordy."

Allie laughed. "Can't wait."

"In the meantime, should you keep your eye out for Jordan? Maybe he needs a friend."

"He'll be making new friends in his new world. There are others like him. I'm sure they'll find each other. He'll be fine until he…"

"Until he what?" Emily's face was tight with her question.

"You know he should go into the light, sweetie. He deserves to go to Heaven."

"So why is he still here?"

"I think Jordan must have made a decision to stay until he could be sure that you'd be all right."

Allie noticed Emily's parents were headed toward them.

"Don't forget to call me if you need anything. I'm a night owl so don't worry about the time. And if you need me to drive to Maryland for a few days, call me," Allie said, squeezing Emily's hand.

"Allie… I have to know something. Did my baby go to Heaven after the accident?"

"Yes, sweetie, he went right away. You'll see him again when it's your time."

"Wait… a boy?"

Allie smiled and pulled back as the ambulance attendants lifted Emily's stretcher into the back of the ambulance. Emily's mother grabbed Allie's arm. She gave her a hug.

"Thank you," Mrs. Paulson whispered. "For everything."

As Mrs. Paulson climbed into the ambulance, Allie noticed someone else was already in the back. Jordan was checking to ensure Emily was secure. He turned and gave Allie a thumbs up.

CHAPTER 13

Present Day

Jordan....

Love... death... forever. That's the story of my life apparently.

So Emily had left the Banks. In my mind, I knew she had to go, but now I am lonelier than I've ever been in my life. Right after the accident, my world was devastated because of my loss of Emily, our baby and... my life.

And then when Emily was in the hospital, I found a way to be near to her again, if only in a small way. Now she is gone and my life is really over. Now I have no one.

Sure I could have hung around Allie, bugging her but it would not have been fair to her. Besides, she was on her way to being a nurse practitioner, and I knew she'd be a damn good one. So while Allie was in school, I was going to leave her be, but I did plan on helping her when she embarked on her new career. Besides, I wanted to convince Allie to shoot bigger and become a doctor. Being a physician was her real calling, she just didn't know it yet.

In the meantime, I made up my mind I was going to make the best of my new dead life, and that would require some hands-on research. Research had always been one of my strong suits. That and evaluation.

And there was something else I wanted to research but didn't dare until I figured out all the rules and restrictions of my dead existence. I didn't want to lose my wife, so I was going to try to… do something.

So since I had loads of free time on my hands, I would start by exploring to see what was what.

What am I supposed to do about my feelings now that I'm dead? My life can't end like this. It just can't.

Wow, I hadn't allowed myself to admit that I was actually dead until now. Dead and buried and the whole nine yards.

Well, it's true. I died a few feet off a highway in North Carolina, not far from my favorite vacation paradise – the Outer Banks.

I am a ghost, and this is my love story.

CHAPTER 14

Jordan's New World....

I had ridden in the ambulance with Emily until it was time to cross the Wright Memorial Bridge. I hopped off then because I wasn't sure what would happen to me if I went any further.

That bridge had always represented two things to me. One – happiness because starting every vacation once I crossed it, I was in the OBX. And two – sadness because once I crossed it going back, vacation was over. In this case, the love of my life was leaving me forever as she crossed that bridge. That bridge would never be the same to me.

As I watched the ambulance drive over the bridge, I said goodbye, not knowing if I'd ever see Emily again. I knew it was for the best but it hurt all the same.

After that, I spent the day walking, well, floating around different parts of Nags Head and Kill Devil Hills. I suppose I was reminiscing about my old life with Emily. I guess you could call it wallowing in self-pity. And I'm okay with that because I was miserable.

That night I found myself at the Dune Burger across from Jeannette's Pier. When I was alive, I loved the place. I'd hit it up at least three times every vacation and grab me a burger, fries and a velvet smooth root beer float.

Ahhhh… now that was Heaven.

And now it seemed awkward to be standing at the walk-up window, staring at the menu, wishing for one last burger. I hadn't eaten anything since the accident, so I pretty much figured that I was done with eating. I couldn't eat a hamburger. Heck, I couldn't even smell the food. Being dead sucks, you know?

But I could do my second favorite thing at the Dune Burger - people watch. I grabbed a seat at one of the picnic tables and sat back to enjoy the show.

Ten minutes in, this older kid on a skateboard came flying by. That guy had his moves perfected, but the adult in me wished he wouldn't be riding in the middle of the road. Minutes later, he flew by again. And again.

The next time he came by, he stopped his board and flipped it up into his hands. Walking over, he stopped and stared at me. I stared back, figuring he was looking at something behind me.

"Hey… Dude," Skate-Boy said.

Whoa, is he talking to me?

"Dude, cat got your tongue?" He stepped closer.

Holy crap, he must be talking to me.

"You can see me?" I asked.

Skate-Boy stepped over and stuck his arm through the side wall of the Dune Burger.

"Yeah, Dude. We are two of a kind. Two dudes, dead to the max."

"I didn't know there were any other…"

"What? Ohhhh… You're newly dead, ain'tcha?"

I looked the kid over. He looked to be maybe 20, not much younger than me, but his demeanor screamed youth. He had on long surfer shorts in a camouflage print, a long-sleeve skater shirt, black fingerless gloves, and high top Chuck Taylor shoes. His hair was surf blown, and he had the slightest of fuzz on his cheeks. The only thing he was missing was a tan.

Was being pale a sign of the dead? Seems a bit cliché.

"I haven't figured much out yet. How'd you end up… you know, like this?"

"Me? Dude, I ride my skateboard in the middle of the street. What are the odds?" Skate-Boy laughed. "Nah, I'm kidding you. One day I was running late, which was a habit I had. Anyway, I was super late for my job interview that day. And I needed to nail that job because Pops had told me I couldn't live at home for free anymore. Anyway, I borrowed my Pop's car and stopped here at the Dune Burger to grab some lunch so I could eat as I drove. Halfway there, I choked on a hot dog. Dude, a hot dog did me in. I used to laugh about a chick… the one who sang… from a long time ago… the one who choked on a ham sandwich and died. Anyway, karma… it always bites you in the butt, ya dig?"

"I got you, all the way! I'm Jordan Snow. Pleased to meet you." Thrilled to meet someone like me, I put out my hand and then pulled it right back, sensing I couldn't shake hands.

"Hey, Jords my man, hit me up," Skate-Boy said, holding his hand in the air for a high-five. "Concentrate real hard and do it, Dude."

Could it be that easy?

I closed my eyes and pulled old meditation habits into play. After I centered myself, I opened my eyes and went for it. The sound of my hand hitting his was muted, but I did it.

Wow.

Skate-Boy grinned. "Dude, I got me a protégé. I'm Luke."

"So do we hang here or…"

"Jords, my man, the world is our oyster," Luke said, nudging me. "Some of our kind are locked to a place or thing but you and me, we hit the dead lottery. We can wander anywhere we want. Maybe it's because of the way you and I died or something."

I must have looked surprised because Luke grinned.

"Yeah, I know how you bit the big one. I'll let you in on a secret… ghosts gossip. Sometimes you learn things you'd rather not have bumping around in your brain, if you know what I mean, and that can be awkward. But most of the time, you catch little nuggets of knowledge. Ya dig? Anyway, because we were traveling at the time of our demise, we can still move around freely. We can also materialize and show ourselves to anyone we want.

"I can see by the look on your face you haven't figured out how to do much yet. We'll get there, Dude. But, my man, you need to be careful with appearing full body. The live ones don't always take kindly to knowing ghosts are around. There's a whole lot of stuff I can teach you."

"You can? I never thought… I mean I hope you can teach me everything quickly. I've got a wife I want to visit. She's up north now. You can teach me the easiest way to get there, right?"

Luke stroked his chin in thought.

"It's possible, but it'll take some planning. Everything we do sucks up our energy. But once we get you juiced up and all, I'm pretty sure you can go for short visits. Nothing special for a while but a visit is a visit, right?"

"When do we start? Is tomorrow too soon for a visit?"

"Whoa, Dude… didn't you hear me say it takes time? You've got ghost feet man, you can't do anything while you still have ghost feet." Luke pointed at my feet.

I looked down. I could see what Luke meant. My feet were shrouded in mist.

Hey, maybe that's why I float as opposed to the whole one foot in front of the other thing.

"Okay, Luke so how do I get rid of these ghost feet?"

"Now comes the fun part. Come on, road trip." Luke grabbed his skateboard and took off.

I stood there for a moment, unsure of what I was supposed to do. When Luke didn't come back, I floated after him. And Luke was flying down the road so it took me a hot minute to catch him. To be honest, I'm pretty sure I caught up because he stopped at a beach house a mile marker past the Blue Moon Beach Grill.

"This is it, Doc. I found this place a while back. Come on. We'll get you some real digits again." Luke said, jumping off his board and taking the stairs two at a time up to the house.

"Wait, you called me Doc."

"Well, yeah, that's what you are, right? You don't stop being a doctor because you died." Not waiting for an answer, Luke glided through the closed front door.

I held back, not wanting to barge into someone's home.

Speaking of which, was anyone home? Would they notice him? But first thing first, will I be able to float through that door like Luke just did?

I didn't know the answers to any of my questions, but the curiosity was killing me, so I floated to the darn door and put out my hand to test it… nothing. The door stopped me flat. I tried again, this time summoning every meditation skill I had ever mastered.

Holy Cow…

First, my arm disappeared into the door, right up to my elbow, and then the rest of me followed.

I was in. Great balls of fire, I was in.

To my surprise, Luke was leaning against the wall, waiting for me.

"Not bad, Doc. Took me longer my first try."

"It didn't even hurt." I touched the door again, my hand went right through it.

So cool.

"So, let's get you some extra energy. The kitchen always has the best supply."

As Luke led the way to the back of the house, I glanced around and noted that the house must be between rentals.

My man Luke is a smart ghost, good to know.

In the kitchen, Luke rummaged around until he found a couple of straws. He handed one to me.

"Now we tap in."

Luke walked over to an outlet on the wall. He squeezed the straw's end until he was able to fit into the spot where you plugged in appliances.

Leaning over, now get this… he was sucking the electricity like he was sucking on a joint. When he pulled back, his hair was standing on end, his eyes were glazed, and he giggled. As I watched, I saw that it took him a couple of minutes to come back to himself, but when he did, he looked almost alive, like flesh and blood real. It was amazing.

"Your turn."

"And you're sure this isn't going to harm us in some way?"

"Harm us? As in kill us? Duuuuude."

Well, I laughed. Luke was one funny dude for sure.

Wait a minute… Dude? Now I was talking like him.

"Okay, here I go." I leaned in for a big hit.

In a few seconds, even the tip of my tongue tingled. I was higher than I had ever been in life. I sucked even harder.

Wham! Lights out!

CHAPTER 15

I came to on the kitchen floor. Every inch of me tingled. I looked at my hands. They glowed. Figuring I shouldn't just lie there, I tried to pull myself into a sitting position. But the room was spinning so I laid back with my eyes closed, hoping the spinning would stop. When I opened my eyes again, Luke was towering over me. He looked concerned which in turn, made me uneasy.

"What happened?" I managed to squeak out.

"Power surge, Doc. It happens every now and again. But check out your down-low digits Doc."

I looked, and sure enough, I could see my feet. I jumped up and hopped from one foot to the other. I couldn't believe it. There they were. I hadn't seen them since the accident, but sure enough, they were there and they were mine. I took a step forward. They were still there. Another step. Still there.

Good golly, Miss Molly…

I decided to walk the length of the hallway.

Oh man, no floating, mama!

Big toe, little toe and all the other toes in between. No fog. No lack of sensation.

I turned to grin at Luke and broke out in a mean tap dance. And I can't dance!

"All right, Mr. Happy Toes. Now, here's the deal. You'll need a maintenance re-charge in a week, maybe two, it depends on you. Everyone's different. If you're going to try something, like making yourself visible to the living, it takes more juice. If you go a distance from here, it takes more juice. If you have conversations with the living, it takes more juice. However, for day-to-day ghostly hauntings, you can float forever, no extra juice needed."

"Are you sure I'm not alive again?"

"Nah, Doc. That's just a high. So… Tomorrow I'm going to take you around to a couple of places where our kind hangs out. Show you who is dope and who to stay away from. But here's the deal, you can't tell any of them about this trick. We have the same sort of problems the living have."

"I can see I've got a lot of the ins and outs to learn."

"Yup… There are those who have some pretty dastardly ways of getting what they want. They like to torment the living. By the way, those living people are called Breathers by our kind. Anyway, they hurt the Breathers, releasing their endorphins into the air for them to snatch. The more they cause harm to a Breather, the more endorphins are released. Sometimes, they go too far, and the Breather dies."

"Wait, go back a step. What are we called?"

"We call ourselves the Living Dead or LDs. I don't know who came up with that name, but it fits. We are dead but still living in a sense, ya dig?"

"LDs… got it. So it's basically like living in the wild west."

"Now you get it. So you can understand that you have to be the one to protect any discoveries you have. Because trust me, no one else will. You have to always keep in the back of your head that many LDs are not like you and I. Basically if a person was a lawbreaker when they died, they are worse as an LD. Many of the LDs from other decades or centuries are pretty bad dudes. The good dead went straight to Heaven in those days. No mistakes like what happened to us."

"But most of those bad LDs are stuck at specific places? So how much harm can they cause?" I asked.

"Plenty. Those LDs are usually tethered to places with a lot of Breather traffic. Restaurants, large vacation rentals, malls, the ferry, that sort of thing. There's some at the hospital, but they usually don't cause many problems for anyone to include the Breathers. Those dudes like to get high on death, and since there is plenty of that in a hospital, they don't have to hurt anyone to get their kicks."

"Crap, I guess I better tell you that my wife and I had tried contacting a ghost at the Black Pelican. T.L. Daniels answered us, or so it seemed anyway. He's not one of the good guys by any chance, is he?"

Well, I now had Luke's full attention. He ran his fingers through his hair, whistling some strange tune.

"Is that a problem, Luke?"

"Big one, Doc. I haven't dealt with him personally, but I do know he's got a lot of rage in him. How'd you try to contact him? Séance?"

"No, just a ghost meter. When we asked if the spirit was T.L., the lights went nuts."

"Well, maybe he won't remember you. Trust me, you don't want his attention."

"So I shouldn't go to the Black Pelican."

"Well, I didn't say that. Like I said, LDs are big gossips. I promise you that they already know you and I met. If you avoid the Pelican, Daniels will go out of his way to get you there. It's better to go and pretend like he's no big deal."

Luke and I sat in the chairs nearest to us. I don't know if we were thinking about the same thing, but I was musing about how I had been foolish to think this whole ghost thing would be easy, that all I had to do was hang out and periodically visit loved ones. Now I could see that it's complicated, very complicated and I suspected more complications were yet to be unearthed.

"So I have some questions. You can't skateboard 24/7 so where do you go? Do I need to find a home or something?"

Luke seemed pleased I was asking questions.

"Yeah, you gotta find a home base. So we talked a little about the LDs who hang out where they are tethered. Those LDs think they don't have a choice. For some reason, they have the idea that if they leave, they'll get lost or eaten by some monster or something. But it's not hurting anyone but them so... Then there's the LDs who hang out in cemeteries. If you like that sort of thing, there's always that option, but it's a little too TV documentary for me. There's also a couple of clubs, so to speak, in what the locals call haunted places. I don't think you'd like the clubs. There is no privacy, and those guys are wild child LDs. No respect for anyone in those hangouts. Plus, the Breathers usually go to those places for ghost hunts, so it's a little chaotic.

"Myself? I prefer peace and quiet. I like the beach. It rejuvenates me. So I usually find places to call home as close to the water as possible. Cubby holes, closets, basements of vacation homes, that sort of thing."

"So you just, like, move in?"

"Pretty much but first you have to find the right place. You want a place where the Breathers are not home much. Homes with dogs are not an option because dogs almost always see LDs. Cats see us too, but they won't make a racket trying to warn their owners. Little kids under five or six see the dead as well so avoid those homes. My preference is a home with a lot of teenagers. They sleep a lot."

Luke's comments had me considering where I could safely chill. He was right about me not liking where all those other LDs hung out. But I didn't think I was ready to find a beach home to make my home base. It occurred to me that the hospital would be perfect for now. You'd think I wouldn't want to be anywhere near a hospital since my dream had been taken from me, but I have loved hospitals since I was a kid. Yes, that would be the perfect living dead home for me.

Suddenly, out of the corner of my eye, I saw something zip past me. It flashed by so quick that I couldn't quite make out what it might be. Thinking it might be a side effect of sucking up electricity, I lightly tapped the side of my head to shake out the cobwebs. But it happened again.

"What was that?" I asked.

"What?"

"I just saw… I think I saw something. It flew past me just enough out of my peripheral vision that I couldn't quite make out what it was. Didn't you see it?"

"Oh, that. Yeah, well don't worry about it. Just ignore it. So did you figure out where to crash for the night?"

"Uh, okay, sure." I stared at Luke, wondering what he wasn't telling me. "I'm going to hang out at the hospital. I guess I'll meet up with you tomorrow. What time is good for you?" I asked.

"Early. I'll introduce you to a few of my friends at the Black Pelican. The ladies there are nice. And don't worry, Daniels doesn't come around until late at night."

Having settled the temporary home question, Luke and I did the shoulder-bump guy thing and went our separate ways.

All the way to my temporary home, all I could think about was that I hoped I didn't see that thing, whatever it was, every time I juiced up.

CHAPTER 16

Early the next morning, I took a leisurely stroll down Virginia Dare Trail to meet up with Luke. I had thought I would get to the Dune Burger earlier than Luke, but he was already waiting for me. I still had a charge from the boost the previous day, so I was ready for our next adventure. Apparently, so was Luke because he dropped a skateboard at my feet the minute I approached.

"I can't ride that." I touched the board with my toe, and it practically flew away on its own.

"Why not? It's not much different than surfing. You surf, right?" Luke asked tucking his hair back behind his ears.

"Uh huh, I'm a car guy. I was planning on getting a new 'Vette once I finished my internship."

"That's dope. Then all you have to do is imagine the board is a convertible with the rag top down. An automatic where all you have to do is concentrate on steering and speed." Luke put one foot on his board and pushed off, leaving me standing on the gravel shoulder of the road.

I gritted my teeth and hopped up on my skateboard. Pushing off, I went… two feet.

Crap, I suck.

I tried again. It took me several attempts before I got going, but pretty soon I was flying up Virginia Dare Trail. Not exactly like a bat out of hell, but fast. I even caught up with Luke. Well, okay, I'm sure I only caught up because he let me. I don't kid myself. I am not an athletic kind of guy. Ever.

As we neared The Black Pelican, I looked at the top windows. For a second, I got a chill.

Was someone looking at me?

Right in front of The Black Pelican, Luke flipped his board into his hands.

I gotta learn how to do that, it's so cool.

Without looking in my direction, Luke gestured for me to follow him. We climbed the stairs that lead from the parking lot overhang and walked into the dining area. It was nearing lunchtime, and the wait staff was setting up the tables as we walked toward the stairs leading to the second level.

I thought I could be cool but just past the hostess stand, my pulse quickened. I knew the moment was coming the minute Luke said we were headed toward the Pelican. But nothing could have prepared me for the invisible hand that squeezed my heart when my eyes lit on the table where Emily and I had dinner on our last visit.

The memory was so fresh that looking away was almost more than I was capable of doing. But somehow I managed to tear my eyes away, telling myself I better catch up with Luke. He had left the dining area, so I walked into the gift shop. I found him there talking to some women who looked like they bought their clothes in the 1800s.

"Dude, what took you so long? Come meet the girls."

As I moved toward them, the younger woman made eye contact with me before lowering her gaze under her thick eyelashes. I must say she was beautiful in an old-fashioned way. She wore her light caramel brown hair on top of her head with loose tendrils around her face. The blouse of her dress was tightly buttoned to her chin, and the skirt below was darkly demure. She was slender and most likely had the legs of a gazelle if you were ever lucky enough to get a glimpse beneath that skirt.

"This is Elise," Luke said, touching her arm. "And this is Maggie." He touched the second woman as well.

Now Maggie was a stunner, but she had a more mature look though I suspect she was only two or three years older than Elise. Hers was more of a sultry beauty. The kind you could look at but if you touched, all hell broke loose. Maggie's clothes were all buttons, brocade, and lace. She had the stature of a queen. Her hair was dark, and like Elise, she had it piled on the top of her head, except her coils of hair looked like they had a mind of their own. Her eyes were the most striking of all, they were the violet color a certain famous actress had. Maggie looked as if she had hidden secrets and desires that were tightly reigned in.

"Pleased to meet you, ladies. I'm Jordan."

Maggie grabbed onto my arm, pulling me into the dining room.

"Let's chat over by the window. We have to keep an eye out for ships. Our husbands are due back any day now."

I shot a glance at Luke, who gave me the 'say nothing' look.

Maggie chose the window with the best ocean view, and the four of us stood there, staring out the window and chatting. Elise stood on the other side of Luke, but I caught her sneaking glances at me.

"My husband's a seafaring man. We have three young ones at home. They've gone to stay at my sister's while I wait for him. Elise's fiancé is on the same ship. It's harder for her than it is for me. This is her first time," Maggie mused.

"I'm sure it is not easy for you either."

"Do you have a wife, Jordan?" Maggie's question perked Elise's ears.

"Yes, but she's gone home to Annapolis, Maryland. She was injured in the accident that killed me."

Both women immediately covered their ears and snap, they vanished.

Luke shook his head. "Ooops… Dude, I forgot to tell you not to mention being dead." He looked at the ceiling. "Don't worry. They'll come back soon, and they'll act as if nothing happened. When they do, play along with them and for goodness sake, don't mention anything about anyone being dead."

"Sorry, man." Realistically, I couldn't have known I would hurt their feelings that way, but I still felt like crap.

And so we waited. Sure enough, fifteen minutes later Maggie and Elise reappeared at the same spots as if they had never left. We continued talking about things, everything except being dead.

By the time early evening came, Maggie and I had become friends. Elise was another story. She had overcome some of her shyness, but she still kept her distance from me as if she was sure I would suddenly bite her if she got too close. Luke later confided in me that I bore a strong resemblance to her fiancé. That certainly put her behavior into perspective.

When it was time for us to leave for the night, Maggie slipped me a book. She put it in my pocket herself as Luke, and I got ready to hit the road. Then we said our goodbyes and the ladies disappeared into the woodwork.

***

On the way to the Dune Burger, we stopped by our favorite empty house and gave ourselves a boost of energy. Luke said I needed to build up my storage capabilities if I wanted to go visit Emily any day soon. After I charged, Luke and I parted ways for the night.

***

Back at the hospital, in the empty janitor's closet, I had found, I settled in a corner and took a look at the book Maggie had given me. It was a handwritten book of poems and prayers. I read a couple of pages and found myself having profound thoughts about my existence, about Emily's possibilities for the future, about everything and anything.

I couldn't tell who had written the book because there was no name on the cover or inside on the first few pages. I was dying to know who the author of the book was because whoever had written the book had real talent.

I wondered, *could Maggie have penned the book?*

If so, it was a shame that she never got published. It got me thinking about what other skills and gifts were buried within my new friends.

CHAPTER 17

At the crack of dawn the next morning, I grabbed my skateboard and made my way to the Dune Burger. Luke was already there.

For a guy that was always late in real life, why is he always early now?

"Dude… you're late. Sleep in?"

I wondered why he was dressed differently than usual. Today, he was wearing knee-length swim shorts and a surfer's tee. A large backpack hung from one shoulder. He was barefoot and leaning against a surfboard.

"Let's have fun today," Luke said.

"I told you yesterday that I don't surf, man, never have, never will. Don't ski or ice skate either. That skateboard of yours was a first for me."

"Dude… I listened. I know you're not a surfer," Luke said as he pointed to a beach chair and umbrella, lying next to his feet. "You can be my cheerleader and watch my backpack while I surf."

Now I don't mind saying I was open to baking in the sun for an afternoon. I hoped it would warm me up. But first, I had a burning question.

"Something's been on my mind, so I have to ask... don't the Breathers see your board? Or your skateboard, for that matter?"

"All questions are good, Doc. And the answer is, nope, as long as you are touching an object, it is invisible to Breathers. Let the thing go and voila! There it is for everyone to see. So, if you get a hold of something important you want to keep for yourself, when you are not using it, hide it where the Breathers aren't likely to stumble across it. And no, your janitor closet is not safe. I like to use abandoned buildings. Still a risk but minimal."

"Good to know."

Luke grabbed his surfboard, shot me a glance before looking toward the ocean and back. I didn't know if I was supposed to read something into his look or not.

"Well, you can't go to the beach dressed in that get-up. You haven't changed your clothes since the accident. They look disgusting by the way. Put your hand on my shoulder," Luke said, offering me his shoulder.

"Why?"

"Because my hands are full."

I rolled my eyes and reached out to put my hand on him. The instant my palm touched Luke's shoulder, he snapped his fingers and bam, we weren't at the Dune Burger anymore.

***

I opened my eyes to see we were in some clothing store that looked familiar to me. The name was on the tip of my tongue, but for the love of me I couldn't spit it out. I grabbed a coffee mug on display and read the price tag.

Right… I was in Emily's favorite store. Gray's Family Department Store.

Glancing around at the store's layout, I was sure it was the one in Kitty Hawk.

"Grab a bag. One of those sales bags will do. No, better make it two. We'll need one bag for those rags you have on so we can throw them in the trash after we finish here. So let's see… you'll need beach clothes and some casual clothes, maybe a couple of t-shirts and shorts. Oh, and we'll have to go somewhere else for jeans and shoes." Luke got busy flipping through some shirts on a rack. He pulled out a shirt and held it to my chest.

"So we grab what we need and not pay for it?"

"Nah… I ain't like that. I leave cash on the register." Luke pulled out another shirt only to discard it for some reason. It looked fine to me, but Luke had a specific image he wanted.

"Where do you get money?"

"I find it." Luke moved on to another rack. I followed close behind.

"But where?"

"Lots of places. On the street, in parking lots, everywhere. Sometimes I take a metal detector and walk the beach after everyone has gone in for the day. You'd be surprised how much money falls out of people's pockets. It's all on the up and up. I don't steal anything."

Who knew ghosts could be so smart?

Luke must not have liked the look on my face because he shook his head and pulled a baggie out of his backpack. It was stuffed with coins and some paper money. Seeing that he could pay, I could relax. I've always had this thing about shoplifters. Dead or not, I wasn't about to become one. I know what you're thinking. I should have kept my mouth shut because I had plenty to worry about being dead and all.

"Now can we get you some better duds? Dude, you need a make-over, like immediately," Luke said with raised eyebrows like I should have known he was an honest ghost.

"Two more questions," I said.

Luke rolled his eyes. I'm sure he couldn't believe his protégé was being such a pain in the butt.

"I know you can see my bloody clothes, right? Well, I saw my face after the accident. It was caved in, man. How come it doesn't look that way anymore? I mean I appeared to a couple of people, and no one's screamed after they got a look at it. And after I juiced up, I caught a glimpse of my reflection. I looked normal, man. No cuts, no bruises, my forehead wasn't crushed anymore."

"Yeah, about that… Well, you and me? We have pride. We don't want anyone to see us like that, so naturally, our spirits project the image we want to present to others. Some ghosts are mad or so screwed up by their deaths that they want people to see the pain they went through. I mean if you see a bullet hole, you know that's gotta hurt, right? Well, they want everyone to see how much it had to have hurt. I never got the whole show your pain thing. I mean what's done is done. You need to make the most of what you have so why not have a pretty face to go with it? So hit me with your next question."

"Okay, I'm dead so why do I need so many clothes? I mean no one can see me so what does it matter?"

"Same premise, Dude. You can't go around in your bloodstained t-shirt. I, for one, don't want to see it. Besides, you never know when someone's gonna see you. You could be lit up, and your wife might happen to walk in the door that second. You want her to see that?"

"No, but—"

"Dude, are you seriously going to tell me you were a slob when you were alive?" Luke cocked an eyebrow at me as he held another shirt to my chest.

It was clear I was losing this argument. I guess I wouldn't want to look at my bloody shirt either.

"You're right. I need some new clothes so I'll pick out a couple of outfits." I threw my hands in the air. "But nothing in yellow. I look like crap in yellow."

Luke chortled. He tried to hide that chortle behind a shirt he was holding at the time, but I heard him all the same.

Now I've never been a shopper, Emily picked out all my clothes. So ten minutes in, I was ready to be done shopping. I went over to a rack displaying shorts and right off the bat found two pairs I liked. I said over my shoulder, "Think you could find some shirts to go with these while I try them on?"

That was all the Luke needed to hear. He jumped into his role as super-shopper to the dead. His fingers literally flew through the racks, throwing shirts this way and that. I hoped he didn't think I was going to pick up that mess. And then a thought popped into my head… maybe he had a finger snap for that too.

***

After I was attired to Luke's satisfaction and we stored my extra clothes in a new hideaway spot Luke had discovered, we headed to the beach. That beach trip taught me a big lesson about hanging on to my possessions while we were mingling with the public.

Luke transported us to a section of beach where the surf was 'tubular.' And then while Luke went to find his nirvana, I put his backpack down and set up my umbrella and chair. I settled back to watch him and the rest of the surfers, both dead and living. Yes, there were others like us. No one came to talk to me, but I could tell which ones didn't have a heartbeat.

Not ten minutes in, I was standing a few feet away from my chair, looking at the waves crashing on shore when I heard someone huffing and puffing. I looked in that direction and saw this rather large woman waddle right up to my chair and umbrella. She took a quick glance around as if looking for the owner. I noticed right away that the woman's eyes were like tiny beads of greed and sweat dripped off her brow. It came to me that I had seen that look before. In the third grade, Byron Reilly was the class bully. He always got that look when he was snatching some kid's lunch money.

Holy crap, she's going to take my stuff.

I hurried over and touching the backpack with my foot, I put my hands on the umbrella and chair when the woman was looking the other way. I have to say the look on her face when she turned to grab her newly found booty was hilarious. Her eyes were shining like new pennies under eyebrows that looked like McDonald's arches, and she was licking her lips. The woman was so eager she tripped over her own feet inches away from my chair and landed on her bum. I cringed because I didn't know if she would crush my now invisible chair. Anyway, she narrowly missed it. I watched her scramble to get to her feet, dust herself off and head back to wherever she had come from.

Whew! I won't forget that lesson.

After that near disaster, I decided I better start acting like an octopus with extra tentacles. I pulled my chair closer to the umbrella, so they were abutted against each other, and Luke's backpack was shoved underneath, touching the chair's legs. Don't ask me how but I managed to sit in the chair without losing my death grip on either the umbrella or chair.

Looking out at the water, my eyes caught sight of Luke sitting on his board, laughing his ass off. I gave him a thumbs up. Then I guess the Devil got a hold of me for a second because I grabbed his backpack and held it out as if I was about to toss it out onto the sand. Luke began to frantically wave at me to stop.

I grinned until I noticed that lady was heading toward my chair again. Shoving the backpack under my chair, I plopped myself down and held onto everything like my life depended on it. I could hear Luke's chortles the entire time. I began to wonder if I was ever going to be good at this whole dead experience.

Having averted disaster, I leaned back in my chair and dug my toes into the sand. I spent the next few hours watching people flying kites and making sand castles. It was nice, almost like I was a Breather again. Luke looked like he was having a great time, too.

I drifted off, daydreaming of my Breather life.

CHAPTER 18

Jordan's Memories...

It was on a Wednesday that I first realized it would be a crime if I didn't spend the rest of my life with Emily. We had moved in together when we entered college but had not made a commitment. We told ourselves that we wanted to see where things led us. We were trying to be responsible adults. But to be honest, we were too tired from school and work and all to think long term. All the same, we were happy.

That day, I had been up for twenty hours straight taking the last of my college exams for the semester and doing a shift at the hospital. By the time I got home, Em was long gone. She was going to have a full day, teaching preschool in the morning and attending afternoon college classes. She had also mentioned earlier in the week that she was going to run over to visit her mother after her classes. So I had my mind set to be alone for several hours, which was okay by me.

Anyway, I walked in the door and dropped my bag on the floor near the front hall closet. Rubbing my sleep-deprived eyes, I walked down the hall to the kitchen. I had my mind set on a cold beer and about two days of sleep.

"Surprise!"

Well, guess what… Emily had organized a birthday party for me. All our friends and family were there. We had a wonderful time. So much so that I forgot how tired I was. Em had planned everything to perfection. There was food, music, even an Elvis impersonator wandering around. Actually, that was my cousin, Pete, but it was a nice touch all the same.

About an hour into the party, Emily led me to the living room where she sat me in a chair in the middle of the room. Our family and friends surrounded me while Emily perched on the corner of my chair and handed me a box wrapped in paper. The paper was illustrated with different models of cars.

"Em, I thought we agreed we weren't going to buy presents until I became a surgeon. Having you in my life is all the present I could ever want anyway."

"I had my fingers crossed, so it doesn't count. And… we all decided that since you've been working so hard, you deserve a special gift," Emily said.

As Em leaned over to kiss me, I gazed into her sparkling blue eyes. They were dancing with excitement. It got me curious as to what exactly was in the box.

I ripped it open. Inside there was… something wrapped like a mummy. I looked at Em, she shrugged. Glancing at the faces surrounding me, all I saw were smiles.

I ripped layer after layer of paper and tape off whatever the object was. It took forever. Finally, I tore my way to the last sheet of wrapping. It wasn't until then that I could feel what it was.

Keys… but to what?

Em jumped up and dragged me from the chair. Now everyone was whispering to each other. We all went outside to see my present.

I was dumbfounded. There, at the curb was a red 1970 Camaro, the car of my dreams. The car I had plastered all over my school binders. The car featured on the poster on my bedroom wall in the fifth grade.

How did she—

I grabbed Em in my arms and whirled her around.

"How… where…" I tried to ask questions, but too many of them were whirling around my head.

"Everyone pooled the money they would have spent on one item for at least a full year. Like Daddy gave up Starbucks for a year. So did your Uncle Paul. For the last five years, every time I went to the grocery store, I kept back twenty dollars. Mom gave up buying books for three years. Your mom gave up massages for two years. Anyway, after we got the money together, it took me about six months of searching to find this car. The color was a perfect match to the one you always said you wanted and the interior was immaculate. I knew it was the one. Like it, Baby?"

"Like it? I love it, Em."

I shouted my thanks to the others, grabbed Em's hand and the two of us took the car for a test drive. As I remember, we didn't come back for hours. I also remember proposing to her for the first time during that ride. It was a magical birthday.

CHAPTER 19

Back to the Present...

"Hey! Sleeping beauty." Luke's voice yanked me back to reality.

"I'm not sleeping. What's the matter? Surf get too rough?" Sometimes, I'm snarky if my dreams get interrupted.

"Good memories, I hope."

"The best. I wish you hadn't snapped me out of it." I shielded my eyes so I could look at him.

"Sorry. Memories are good to have, but we need to get going." Luke tapped his foot impatiently.

"Why?"

"Tonight, some pirate ghosts will be taking over the shoreline for five miles either way," Luke nudged my foot to get me up.

"I'd like to watch some pirate action."

It sounds like fun to me. What's the big deal?

"Uh, no, Dude… not fun at all. Those are dangerous ghosts. Not to Breathers, but to us. Most of them have been dead for centuries. And remember, they… are… pirates. Swashbuckling, pillaging, destroying everything in sight pirates."

"No fun pirates like at The Jolly Roger?" Luke shook his head. "All right then I want you to teach me your finger snapping thingy."

Luke stuck the foot of his surfboard into the sand and leaned against it. By the serious look on his face, he was about to tell me something interesting.

"Look, the other day you told me you saw something when we juiced up."

"That shadow thing. I still don't know if I actually saw anything or not."

Luke cocked his head and stared at me for a moment almost as if he didn't know if he should tell me or not. I was about to say forget it, that it was just my imagination when he finally spoke.

"I think it's time to warn you about the shadow people. That thing you saw was one of them. You want to avoid shadow people at all costs. I was hoping they'd leave you alone, but they always look at the new ones as fresh meat."

"Now you're scaring me. What do you mean by fresh meat?"

"Shadow people are like vampires to the newly dead. They have sub-zero power, so they want to take yours."

"Crap."

"Crap is right, Dude. They creep up on you and torment you until you give in. Whatever you do, don't give in. They will suck you dry until you are like a zombie and then continue to feed until you become a shadow person like them. The biggest problem is that they are so hungry for power that they don't know when to quit."

"Wait. You can't just throw out the vampire word like that. Or zombie for that matter. Are you serious? I'm too new at this for you to mess with my head like that."

Well, I think I made Luke mad because he leaned over and got in my face.

"I'm not trying to mess with you, Dude. I'm trying to warn you. You best take this seriously. They will destroy you if given a chance." Luke calmed down a bit and continued, "But if you don't interact with them, they can't get in your head. And if they can't get in your head, you won't give them permission to drain you. Got it?"

"Man, this whole dead thing has too many twists and turns. Just when I think I'm getting a handle on things you throw in something new."

"I hear you, but this is who you are now. Look, just remember that shadow people have to have your permission to drain your energy. Don't interact with them and you'll be fine."

I looked out at the ocean waves crashing on the shore and wondered if I could have become one of them. I rubbed my face with my hands, squirming inside at the possibilities. For the first time since I died, I was scared. No, I was terrified. Could I still become one of them?

"So how do these vampire/shadow people come to be?"

"Most shadow people were broken people in life. A lot of times, they were rule breakers with no regard for others. So when they die, they continue that same behavior and become shadow people."

"How will I know which rules I can't break?"

"I told you, they were broken people in real life. The rules they break in death are things like addiction and causing harm to the LDs. You were never broken, and you aren't a rule breaker, so you are safe as long as you stay away from them. Don't look at me like that."

Luke had caught me with my naked face on. I was worried that I must have become broken after the accident in some way and it was only a matter of time for me. I averted my eyes, I suppose that didn't help.

"Oh that's right, you're a science guy. Okay, hear me out. So... the guy you saw in the charging house... his name is Edward. I met him when I was new as well, so I was a bit naïve back then. Anyway, I took him to charge up, and he wasn't satisfied with the results, so he poured a gallon of water on the floor in front of the receptacle and then stood in the water as he juiced up. He electrocuted himself to get a more intense high. I warned him not to do that, but he didn't listen. He just did what he wanted. Three times that I know of. The last time, he blew out every cell in his body. One minute he was glowing like a firebug on cocaine and the next, he was nothing more than dust in the air. Now he's a shadow dude."

"Holy crap!"

"Nothing holy about it, Dude. I should have listened to him right from the jump. He said he died when a drug dealer shot him with a twelve gauge for stealing dope. That didn't bother me at the time. I always thought that everyone should be forgiven at least once in life, right? But he was telling me who he was… inside. He was a junkie. Drugs in real life, electricity in this one. He didn't treasure his new chance. Instead, he wasted it to get high. Now, do you understand when I say you are not like them?"

"I do but—"

"Look, it's simple. When you think you see a shadow person, ignore them. Don't let them in and they can't touch you. Got it?" Luke stared at me, I could see he was serious.

"Don't look. Don't listen. Got it."

"Good, now we better get going. Pirates, remember?"

We began the long trek back to the Dune Burger. I didn't even notice when Luke touched my shoulder. BAM, we were at the vacant house. I had forgotten that it was time for us to recharge. I wondered if Edward would be watching. Then I decided it didn't matter. I wasn't going to let a shadow person get in my way. I was determined to master this dead thing so I could see Emily again.

CHAPTER 20

"You're on your own today, Doc," Luke said, walking out to the street.

"Bummer... I wanted you to teach me some more tricks." I scratched my head.

I was getting anxious to check on Emily. But as Luke kept reminding me, I wasn't ready yet. I had more to learn before I could chance going so far away.

"Sorry but there's something I need to do. We'll work on your LD education later on. In the meantime, practice your transporting skills. Until you can transport accurately, you aren't ready to travel distances. I know you are anxious to go to Emily, but if you want it to be a successful trip, you should wait until you have mastered the basics." Luke turned and made eye contact with me to show me he was serious.

He was right. I didn't have to like it, but he was right. While I had come to learn that the finger-snapping trick I admired so much was actually called transporting, I hadn't been able to get it to work like I wanted it to. Sometimes, I transported to odd, unexpected places. Once I landed in the ladies room of some gas station in New Jersey. Thank goodness no one was in it at the time. I needed practice and a lot of it.

As I watched Luke skate away, I wondered why he was so secretive today. Sometimes he was an open book and others… well, the guy could clean up if he played poker. Maybe I was still proving myself to him. I had so many questions and so few answers.

To tell the truth, I knew he didn't have to account for his time or anything else. I knew that what Luke did was none of my business. I guess that it was the whole dead thing that made me feel so insecure. Well, I would just have to pull up my big boy britches and do what I needed to do.

Once Luke was out of my eyesight, I set about figuring out what to do with myself for the day. For the first hour, I spent my time at the Dune Burger, watching the people and creating stories about their lives. It was an activity Em, and I had loved to play when I was… alive.

Em…. Ummmmm, I better not go there.

After I got tired of people watching, I went to work on my transporting skills. Luke was right. I had been avoiding trying it again because of what had happened the last time. I set my mind to work on it until I could do it the right way. I had never been a quitter, and

I wasn't about to start now. I jumped to my feet, psyched myself up and came up with a place I wanted to go. I snapped my fingers. Nothing happened.

I tried again. This time I found myself behind the Dune Burger, scaring the crap out of a stray dog digging in the trash.

Hmmm, not what I wanted.

I tried again. This time I landed across the street in the exact spot I had shot for. It gave me chills. I tried a few more places. Our vacant house. My closet. All successes.

Yay!

But I still didn't feel I had the transporting process down pat yet. I wanted to ask Luke more questions before I did something permanent I couldn't reverse. Deciding to put my practice on hold for the moment and do some visiting, I grabbed some trinkets I had gathered for Elise and Maggie. I was going to skateboard to the Pelican but told myself it wouldn't do anyone any harm if I transported one more time.

***

Well, my transporting didn't exactly turn out how I expected. I was shooting for the main dining room but landed in the kitchen where I found myself behind Elise and Maggie who were busy whispering in the chef's ear. It was funny to watch.

First, Elise whispered in the chef's left ear. Shrugging his shoulder as if it somehow helped, he swatted at the buzzing. Then Maggie whispered in his right ear. He slapped at his ear again. When they whispered at the same time, he grunted in frustration and threw his apron on the table before stomping from the room.

"Now ladies, you are going to drive the poor man crazy."

Maggie and Elise turned, saw me and shrieked in unison as they rushed to greet me. Each took one of my arms and yammered at me. About what, I do not know because their voices canceled the other out. So I waited them out. After a bit they finally stopped to gulp in some air, I jumped in.

"Ladies, ladies, I hoped we could have a fun afternoon. What would you like to do?"

"Old Maid," they squealed in unison.

"What is that?"

"A card game, silly," Elise offered as she blushed as bright as a strawberry.

I didn't know how to play Old Maid, but it didn't matter to them. They insisted it was an easy game to learn and they would teach me. Maggie pushed me toward their favorite table and magically pulled a deck of old looking cards from her pocket. She slapped them on the table and pointed to a chair, which I obediently took. Elise sat opposite Maggie with me to her right. The minute Maggie began dealing the cards like a riverboat gambler, I knew I was in trouble. Twenty minutes in, I lost the first game.

"I want you to know I am claiming you as my fiancée's brother," Elise announced.

I looked at Maggie, raising my eyebrows. She leaned in toward me, whispering, "So she can look at you without guilt, sir."

Thank goodness. Now maybe we can be friends.

"I am most honored, Elise."

"Mr. Jordan, are you married?" Elise asked, demurely eyeing me over her cards.

"It's Jordan. We're family, remember? My wife's name is Emily. I call her Em. She's as beautiful as she is smart."

"Too bad you're dead," Maggie said.

I stared at her, taking in her words.

"We've decided it's silly to pretend we are alive," Maggie continued.

Elise bobbed her head, agreeing. "Silly, silly, silly."

Maggie shot her a look, and Elise quickly looked at her cards.

I placed a photo on the table.

"This is my love. I slipped this from my wallet after the accident before the police turned my items over to Em. It was the only way I could get a photo of her."

The ladies oohed and awed, each taking turns touching the edges of Emily's photo.

"She's lovely, Jordan," Maggie said. "I wish I had something of my Richard."

Elise patted her hand, "As do I, sweet Maggie."

Suddenly, some dark thing began to buzz around me. Out of the corner of my eye, I could almost see a shadow.

Nah, not here.

I swatted at the buzz that was near my ear now. The shadow figure edged into my peripheral vision.

Maggie noticed me slapping at my ear first. She nudged Elise who began to giggle.

"Edna Jean," they chortled in unison.

"What?" I asked, getting annoyed that the gnat or whatever it was wouldn't leave me alone.

"That's Edna Jean trying to get your attention. Just ignore her, and she'll stop," Maggie proclaimed.

"She's a shadow person?"

"Unfortunately she is. Elise and I stood next to her on the widow's walk for months."

"What happened to her?"

"Oh, she was not very nice. Not at all." Elise murmured before covering her mouth in shame. Maggie patted her hand.

"I agree, she wasn't very nice. I think it was because she was touched in the head, the poor thing. First, she lost her husband to black lung disease while her son was at sea. He was only sick for three weeks before he perished. And then, the ship her son was on was lost at sea. It was said the pirates boarded the ship and murdered everyone but no one knew for sure.

"Her grief ripped her soul apart. After the deaths, she totally lost her last piece of sanity and she hung herself from the railing on the widow's walk with her face pointed toward the sea. Elise and I were still alive, but we knew she was still here, with us, waiting."

"That must have been a terrible time for you and Elise. So very sad."

The ladies dabbed at their eyes with some lacy handkerchiefs they produced from out of thin air.

"One day, long after Edna Jean perished, some out-of-state people, strangers really, came to the Pelican to hold a séance. They were looking for... for another soul, but Edna Jean showed up," Maggie said.

"And you were there?" I asked, unable to think of any other question.

"What those people were doing was against God's rules. No, we did not participate, we stood in the corners with our ears covered. The people asked questions, and Edna Jean kept rattling on about her son, so her answers made no sense to them. After a while, the people tried to end the séance, but Edna Jean wasn't ready to let go. She got so riled up and angry that her eyes were crazed and there was spittle on her chin."

"It was most terrible," Elise piped in.

"Every time one of the séance people tried to stand up, Edna Jean pushed them back into their chairs. The séance people got scared, and Edna Jean got angrier. Eventually, her head exploded. Literally. Needless to say, the séance people couldn't see that, but they could feel the explosion. It blew a couple of them out of their seats. Ever since then, Edna Jean's been a shadow person," Maggie finished.

"She is always stealing our hairpins. I don't know what for, it's not like she has a head." Elise sniffed.

Maggie put her hand on Elise's and said, "We feel sorry for her. Once she was a good woman, who loved her husband and son more than life itself."

Elise nodded.

"I was told there was someone else who hung out at the Pelican. His name is T.L. Daniels—" I didn't get to finish my sentence because Elise's hands flew to cover her face and Maggie looked stricken as if I had summoned a monster.

"Don't say his name," Maggie hissed at me.

"Why? What's he gonna do? Smack me?"

"He might. He gets angry. So angry. Maybe he didn't hear you. I don't hear him coming."

We all sat there, waiting. He never came so I guess Daniels didn't hear me mention his name but the afternoon was over.

I said my goodbyes and said I'd come by another day. But first I wanted to master their Old Maid card game. The ladies were giggling when I left, but I could also see some fear in their eyes. I didn't know if that meant that T.L. would be coming to reprimand them after I left.

CHAPTER 21

The next day found me at the library, researching T.L. Daniels. Luke came with me, but he didn't support my interest in knowing more about Daniels.

"Check this out. There's more than one story about what happened. And this Captain James Hobbs, the Station Keeper? I don't know, but maybe Daniels was not the bad guy they claimed. Daniels had reported Hobbs to his superiors for using government-owned paint on his personal boat. But other accounts said Daniels may have insulted or accidentally spit tobacco on Hobbs' wife."

"Well, he is an angry spirit."

"Maybe it's because he was wronged. They claim he wanted Hobbs' job as Station Keeper but if that's the case, why would he go about trying to get it by insulting Hobbs' wife? To me, it sounds like something Hobbs either lied about or exaggerated to booster his indignant position when he got caught using the paint. Maybe it was just an excuse to cover what he planned to do in retaliation."

"During their time period, insulting someone's wife was paramount to besmirching a man's reputation, and a man's reputation was his most valuable possession." Luke stood by the window, watching the traffic roaring by. "I wish those cars would slow down. We're going to have a new buddy if they don't."

"Some of these records claim Daniels pulled a gun first but others indicate there were no witnesses, so who is right? Plus Hobbs shot Daniels more than once with a shotgun. He made sure Daniels couldn't report him again."

"Daniels was armed, right?"

I leaned back in my chair, staring at Luke. "He had a pistol on him."

"So I'll ask again. How can you jump to the conclusion that Hobbs was not shooting in self-defense? Is it clear who shot first?"

"What's clear is that Hobbs shot Daniels twice with a shotgun. And nobody was in the room except the two of them. Most of the reports state the men clashed all the time. And there are the conflicting stories of what caused the shooting to happen in the first place. It's awfully convenient to claim Daniels had not been a gentleman to Hobbs' wife. It looks to me like Daniels was set up."

"And I would say we will never know the full truth. Are you done researching Daniels now?"

"There's nothing else to find, so yes, I'm done. You know, there's this thing in America about being innocent until you're proven guilty. I'm going to treat Daniels as an innocent person until he does something to make me think otherwise."

"I can't tell you what to do," Luke said, shaking his head. "But I will tell you this… you best make sure he's trustworthy before you go giving him your trust."

"I'm still testing you, aren't I?"

Luke did a double take which was precisely the reaction I wanted. I put my arm around his shoulders and snapped my fingers.

And with that snap, we were at our favorite vacant house except apparently someone had moved in. We almost landed on the family dog. I don't know who yelped louder, the dog or myself. I quickly snapped my fingers, and we were at the Dune Burger. But there we discovered it was 'take your dog out for a burger' night, and we set off a firestorm of yowling with our pop-in. Not good.

Snap! We were in my closet at the hospital.

"Sorry. Got any idea where we should go? I'm due for a recharge."

"I already found us a new place."

"Why didn't you say so before I ran us all over the OBX?" I guess I sounded testy, but I was a little frustrated at the moment.

"Practice, practice, practice," Luke said as he grabbed my arm and snapped his fingers.

CHAPTER 22

Luke was busy again on Thursday, so I grabbed my latest bag of goodies and transported to The Black Pelican.

When I popped in, the place was empty except for one waitress who was polishing silverware at a table near the front desk. I walked over because I wanted to see the spot where T.L. had died. Yes, I was calling him T.L. now.

The dark discolored area on the wooden floor near the hostess stand sent chills up my spine. I spent some time there, imagining that tragic day, wondering who was right. After several minutes, I tired of that and went looking for the girls.

I found them in the kitchen arguing over the fresh produce spread out on the main cutting board table.

"Ladies, ladies… what in the world are you arguing about?"

Both women turned toward me, their eyes blazing. The minute they saw it was me, they grinned and rushed over to touch me. It wasn't an inappropriate touching, but it was surprising. I guess they were starving for male attention.

I wondered if T.L. ever played cards with the ladies or even had casual chit-chats with them. I suppose I sound a bit obsessed with him, but I swear I am not, I'm merely curious.

"It's nothing really. Sometimes, we get bored and… one thing leads to another, and we fall into bickering over the silliest of things," Maggie said, with Elise bobbing her head in the background.

"I see. Well, how about I give you something to be happy about? I come bearing gifts, but first let's retire to the upstairs. I know he can't hear us," I said, pointing to the chef. "But I don't like noisy kitchens."

When they know they are getting a gift, they are all the same no matter when they were born. Maggie and Elise grabbed each other's hands. They were so excited they could barely contain themselves. I'll admit it, their peals of laughing glee brought a beaming smile to my face.

The ladies ran up the stairs, hand in hand. I followed, holding back in the doorway. I had something important to say to Edna Jean.

"Edna Jean, please allow me to visit with the ladies without you buzzing around my head. I appreciate your situation, but I cannot do anything to help you right now. I hope to discover a way to help you sometime in the future. All I can do is tell you how sorry I am for your loss. Thank you."

I don't know if it worked or if Edna Jean didn't happen to be around that day, but as requested, my shadow girl did not buzz me that night.

Yes, I know that Luke warned me about having contact with the shadow people, but you see, I am a healer. That is why I became a doctor and wanted to become a surgeon. I was a healer. After re-reading the book that Maggie had given me, I decided to find out if I could heal shadow people too.

***

Back to the Ladies...

By the time I entered the room, Maggie and Elise were almost in control of themselves. I pulled out my bag of goodies and handed them each a bottle of fragrance and some shiny nail polish. I had been on the fence about the perfume, but Luke assured me we ghosts can smell things if we choose to do so. I wish I had known that all the times I had hung out at the Dune Burger, but I'm glad I listened to him because the ladies were thrilled. The nail polish was a hit right off the bat, too.

As usual, I had bitten off more than I could chew because Maggie had a request.

"Sir, will you do me the honor?"

My mind went racing. *Did Maggie want a manicure?*

As it turned out, that would have been a pleasure. Nope, Maggie wanted a pedicure, and Elise wanted one too. It seems they had seen them on the tourists who came to The Black Pelican and had secretly coveted painted toenails ever since.

I had to oblige. Gentlemen always accommodate the wishes of women. It was a rule somewhere.

Why, oh why, did I bring the polish?

"Maggie, have a seat," I said, leading Maggie to a comfortable chair.

Before I got started on the pedicure, I said, "First, let me give you the rest of your gifts. For you, Maggie. I have new Old Maid cards and another game called Go Fish. For you, Elise, I have some magazines and a handful of shiny hair clips."

Well, my ladies swooned.

Oh, my God, I can't believe I used that word in a sentence. My dead life was changing my vocabulary.

Absorbed with studying her new cards, Maggie was sitting relatively still in her chair. I decided that I better just dive in and get it over with. So I found a cushion and sat on the floor in front of her. That's when things started to go south. When I slipped off her shoes, the smell could have knocked me over.

I didn't want to hurt Maggie's feelings but I had to do something quick, or I'd be barfing all over her feet. Racking my brain for something to kill the stink, I remembered I had some old peppermint-flavored Chapstick of Emily's in my pocket. I turned so Maggie couldn't see me and shoved a piece of the Chapstick into each nostril. Trust me, it's no fun having Chapstick up your nose, but it sure beat the smell wafting from Maggie's feet.

Once I had Chapstick securely up my nose, I was ready to dive in again. I got my first peek at her toes when I pulled her socks off.

Good golly, they are so gross.

The woman had apparently never had anyone give her a pedicure, ever. It was a good thing I had thought to bring a nail kit. It took me a good hour and a half, but when I was done, I have to say her little piggies were adorable.

Elise wanted me to start on hers right away but I couldn't. No way. I had to take a break first. I don't know how those professional nail people do it but they are saints in my mind.

I mean... ewwwwwww.

Anyway, I sat back in a chair and enjoyed watching them coo over their gifts while I relaxed. It was like watching orphans who had never had a Christmas tree before. And it made me wonder how long it had been since a man gave them presents. It kinda made me sad inside, so I made up my mind to bring little offerings more often. After all, everyone deserves to feel special from time to time.

After a few minutes, I convinced myself that I could get through it. I got Elise seated and began to remove her slippers. I figured her toes were in the same condition. I was right. Thankfully, I still had more Chapstick in my pocket.

Unfortunately, Elise had another issue. She had some pretty impressive looking bunions. It was no wonder the ladies had been jealous of the tourists' toes. Poor girl would never make it as a foot model. Somehow I managed to keep a smile on my face and got to work.

"Oh, Jordan. Thank you." Elise wiggled her toes and jumped to her feet the minute I was done, dancing around on her tippy toes.

"Now ladies, you have to let the polish completely dry before you put your shoes back on."

A loud bang startled the three of us. We all turned to look at the same time. There, standing in the doorway was a man. An impressively mean looking guy. His clothing was 1800s all the way. The crash we heard came when the man threw the door open and slammed it against the wall.

Holy crap, it's T.L. Daniels himself.

Maggie and Elise gasped and disappeared. Meanwhile, T.L. shot me a death stare.

"Sir, what business brings you here?"

"Business?" Good lord, his tone made it sound as if I had come looking for a fight. Now, I'm not a fighter, so I was concerned.

"Are you one of Hobbs spies?" T.L. marched straight at me. I had to back up in a hurry to keep out of harm's way.

"No, no. I came to see Maggie and Elise. They were here a minute ago."

"I doubt you, sir. You best not have come here to cause me harm."

"I assure you, I have good intentions. I'd like to introduce myself. My name is Jordan Snow." I held out my hand to shake, but he eyed me suspiciously.

"Theopolis Daniels. I was a surf-man until a dastardly... until I was shot down in cold blood. How were you murdered, sir?" T.L.

circled around me, scrutinizing every inch of me. I had to keep twisting so I could see his face.

"May I call you, T.L.?"

T.L. didn't answer in a real way. Instead, he continued circling me.

"Okay… well, T.L., I was not murdered, I died in a car accident."

T.L. stopped in front of me and crossed his arms in front of me. "I do not believe I am familiar with that… 'car' word. Is it a vessel or a carriage?"

"We use them to get around. Cars are a mechanical means of transportation. Do you ever look out the window and see mechanical objects moving by?"

"I have not. I am confined to this place and cannot view the road. I can observe the sea at times but nothing below."

"I'm sorry you can't experience the world outside of this place."

T.L. scrutinized my face as if he could see deep into my soul. By the dark, brooding look on his face, I couldn't tell if he was friend or foe.

"And what happened to end your life, sir?"

"Another car hit my Camaro head on. That's the type of car I was driving, a Camaro. I died quickly because my aorta was severed. Ironic since I was going to be a heart surgeon."

Wow, I can't believe I said that out loud.

"You use many strange words." T.L. got in my face again to sniff at me this time. "But then again, you are a pretty boy."

I frowned. *Pretty boy? Was he insulting me?*

"I was shot by a cowardly bastard. Three times. It was not a fair fight. In fact, my murderer tricked me. I didn't have a chance. All of them lied. Even Hobbs' woman. And then they colluded to ruin my reputation. The bastards."

"I believe you. Can we start over?" I held my hand out. He didn't take my hand but he did give me a slight nod.

"I gave the ladies some gifts, but I didn't forget about you. I read somewhere that you liked fine whiskey." I handed the bottle I brought to T.L. "I know you don't eat but I wasn't sure if you could drink."

T.L. held the bottle to the light, flipping it over in his hands a few times before turning to stare at me.

"You wouldn't try to poison me, would you?"

"Now T.L., we're both dead, right? I can't kill you."

And poof, he disappeared.

Geez, another one who doesn't want to acknowledge he's dead.

I waited for a few minutes, but no one came back, not even the ladies. Since they weren't returning, I transported back to the Dune Burger. I'm proud to say I made it on the first try.

CHAPTER 23

Sunday was my birthday. At least I think it was my birthday. I've been losing track of time since I had died. Maggie told me it was to be expected. She said it seemed like just last month when she had stood at the dock, waving as her husband had sailed off into the Atlantic.

Anyway, once Maggie and Elise got their minds set on something, that was it. And so Luke and I were told it was mandatory we celebrate our birthdays. Mine would be the first. Because the ladies were stuck at The Black Pelican, it was decided we would have the party there. Maggie said there was an upstairs room that was seldom used that would be perfect for our little party.

But I was worried. I don't know why but a nagging thought told me it wasn't going to turn out the way anyone thought.

***

Luke and I arrived at the Pelican on time as requested and entered through the front door. The downstairs dining area was packed which was no big deal until Luke shot me a glance. Shaking my head, I knew exactly what he was thinking. You see my man was a trickster. Nothing mean, just shaking-your-head-silly kind of pranks.

I stood in the doorway watching him move things on people's plates and tables. He tickled people's necks and kissed cheeks. And then I watched as he played a prank on one poor, elderly lady who reached for her water glass only to have it disappear right in front of her eyes. It vanished because Luke put his finger on it. Like I said, silly stuff.

I let him have a few more minutes of fun because no one was getting hurt or anything. I didn't mind it when he touched people on the shoulder, making them turn to look for a culprit. And even though I thought he was crossing a line, I didn't object when he began to put people's eyeglasses into their water glasses. But he went too far when he levitated one unfortunate guest's full dinner plate. Enough was enough. Grabbing his arm, I dragged him to the stairs.

As we moved toward the stairs, out of the blue, one of the diners shouted, "Ghost," and jumped to his feet, pointing at us.

Heads were bobbing as diners whipped out cameras and cell phones while the wait staff searched under tables and behind plants, looking for ghosts. More specifically – for us.

Well, I didn't know how to handle the uproar. I wasn't used to being hunted as a ghost. I dashed across the room and made for the stairs. I took a running jump up the staircase, my feet barely touching any of the steps. I didn't notice Luke had transported.

***

I raced down the hall to the room where we were having my party and tore open the door.

"Surprise!"

You could have knocked me over with a feather, I was floored. The room was large, and inside there were two dozen or more ghosts to include Maggie and Elise. My tongue was tied.

"Happy Birthday!" Luke shouted from my side. "Don't you think I did a great job keeping you occupied until everyone arrived?"

I slowly turned to look at him. "You showed yourself, didn't you?"

Luke didn't have to say a word. The smirk on his face said it all. I had been tricked by the best. I got over being played when I remembered it was my birthday party.

Woot! Woot!

I looked around at all the faces staring back at me. Some I had seen in our travels up and down Virginia Dare Trail, others I had never seen before. I even caught a glimpse of Edna Jean standing in the corner, she flickered in and out so I could barely see her face but I knew it was her. I smiled, curiously enough she smiled back and then disappeared.

Right after that, Maggie came over and stepped between us to take my arm and escort me around the room, introducing me to some of the other ghosts.

There was a young lady from the Croatan Inn, she seemed shy but sweet. And Maggie tried to introduce me to some playful children from The White Doe Inn in Manteo, but they were too hyper to pay attention to me.

I have to say some of the ghosts seemed standoffish, while others were chatty and oblivious to allowing others to get a word in edgewise. It was an odd gathering, to say the least. Shortly after introductions, some of our guests began to fade out.

I turned to Luke, figuring he would know what was going on.

"Most ghosts here aren't free like you and I. Even Maggie and Elise can only leave the Inn for a few minutes at a time. It takes every bit of energy they can pull together to pop in and out. But Maggie and Elise put the word out that they were expected to come and welcome you because it was your birthday and so they came. I helped transport a few who were unable to do it by themselves."

"That makes me sad."

"There's no need to be sad. Those ghosts got out for a few minutes and got to see somewhere other than their haunts."

I glanced around the room and noticed T.L. He was standing in a corner by himself. I gave him a polite nod of acknowledgment which he returned. But neither of us moved toward the other. I figured he needed more time to accept my friendship.

To my surprise, I watched a lady approach T.L. with a baby. She was young and comely. She was wearing a charming frock of a dark pink silk. I caught a glimpse of her feet. She wore those high top shoes that had buttons all up the side. Very fashionable for the times. Her baby was swaddled in white lace and wool. T.L. took the young lady's hand and kissed her fingertips, then cooed over the baby. They made a striking couple. Seconds later, she vanished.

"I didn't know T.L. had a baby. I don't remember reading anything about her."

"Margaret had the baby after he was buried at sea. She took the baby and went to live with her family in New York. I'm afraid it didn't end well for her. Margaret and her son were killed during a home invasion. Their spirits are tied to New York so he seldom gets to see her."

"Why didn't she and the baby enter Heaven?" I had my eye on T.L. again. When his family was here, T.L. had looked like a loving family man. Now his face was tight with anger and disappointment.

"Margaret chose to stay on earth because her father was horribly maimed in the attack He lingered in the hospital for months. Margaret wanted to go with her father when the time came, but when the angels came for him, she wasn't there. She had transported here to say goodbye to her husband. It was a tragic situation for her. Now it seems she and the baby will walk the earth, most likely for eternity."

I glanced over at T.L. again, but he was gone. Maggie and Elise grabbed my arms and escorted me to a chair where they both pushed me down onto the seat.

"It's time to open your gifts," Maggie announced in a voice brimming with excitement.

Maggie handed me an item wrapped in newspaper and string. I opened it. It was a hand-painted portrait of Emily. Immediately, a lump in my throat threatened to choke me. I had shoved my loneliness for her down deep somewhere inside me, now it came bursting forth in the form of hot tears. I wiped them away with the back of my hand.

Now I'm crying like Emily. Good grief.

"I... I... I love it, Maggie. It's perfect." I choked out.

Maggie beamed and nudged Elise who pulled a similar wrapped item from behind her. She handed me the package and blushed.

I carefully opened it. Inside, was a suit vest. I had seen one like it on T.L. Not my style but like my mother was always sure to say, 'you should always accept birthday gifts graciously.' I stood up and tried it on. It was made of rough cotton and had pinstripes and gold buttons. It fit me perfectly.

"It was my Lance's. I hope you don't mind. He seldom wore it. Oh... I should have given you something else. I'm sorry," Elise said with a worried look on her face.

"No, I love it, Elise. I will cherish it. I promise you." I reached out and took her hand to reassure her.

Elise dipped in a curtsy. I was relieved to see that the look on her face had slipped back into one of happiness.

Next, Luke stood in front of me.

"My turn," he said, but his hands were empty.

I must have had a stunned look because he put his hands on either side of my face and cupped my cheeks.

"It's time for you to go visit with your wife. My gift is that I will prepare you for your trip. If you still want to go, that is."

Well, I've never held a man in my arms and danced before, but that's precisely what I did. And Luke didn't pull back. I know my hugs were crushing, but he smiled and allowed me to express my joy. Then the ladies rushed over, and we had a group hug. My happiness was complete.

It was the best night of my dead life yet.

CHAPTER 24

The First Visit...

Luke said I should keep my first visit to Maryland short. I complained, but he said I could always come back again and lengthen the time I spent there each time. Reluctantly, I agreed.

He also advised me to take certain precautions while I was in Maryland but to be honest, I almost blew it in my first five minutes.

Don't tell him, okay?

You see I was so excited that I transported dab smack in the middle of Emily's hospital room, fully charged, viewable by anyone looking my way. Thankfully, Emily was asleep, and no one else was in the area.

After I got a grip on myself, I packaged my energy in my safe place deep inside me. Then walking over to Emily's bed, I stared at her for several minutes, soaking in every in. I was dying to find out her medical status, so I grabbed her medical chart from the end of the bed and scanned every page. It seemed Emily had had back surgery early the week before and was recovering nicely. And she was scheduled for therapy later in the day. One day soon she was going to be as good as new.

I climbed onto the bed beside her and draped my arm across her chest. She smiled in her sleep and seemed to pull me closer, except I knew that was impossible in my current state. So I put my head on her shoulder and pulled as close as I could get without actually entering her body. Her breathing became even and deep like it always had when we… when I was alive.

We stayed that way for two hours. Sure, I knew I was pushing my time limit, but how bad could it be that I wanted a little time with my love?

Don't even say it, I knew I was kidding myself. And I knew I should be conservative. But I love Em so much.

After a bit, the door opened, and a therapy technician came in. I could tell she was a therapy tech because most ones I knew had a certain walk when they entered room. Her name tag said she was Kristen. I didn't like her. Don't ask me why. Looking back, I'm sure it was because she got to spend more time with Em that I did. Yes, I was most likely jealous.

Anyway, Kristen reviewed Emily's chart. Walking to the side of the bed, she checked Em's vitals, recording her findings.

During the exam, Emily opened her eyes and grinned. For a brief instant, she seemed to be smiling at me.

"I had the most wonderful dream, Kristen. Jordan and I were hugging and loving each other," Emily purred.

I noticed a tightening of Kristen's eyebrows.

There! I knew there was something about that girl. What is her problem?

"What's wrong?" Emily asked

That's my girl. Challenge her.

"Nothing. So are you ready to get on those legs again?"

Liar. Never lie to your patient.

I jumped off the bed and stood over near the door. Kristen pulled a nearby wheelchair close to the bed, probably as a precaution. Walking to the side of the bed, she helped Emily roll onto her side and swing her legs over the side of the bed. Then, Kristen held onto Emily's hands as Em tried to stand. Emily looked like she was going to buckle, but Kirsten held tight. I looked at Kirsten's face. Her eyes were warm and embracing if that's possible.

Whoa… she looks like she cares about Emily.

I rushed over and pressed myself against Em's back to help stabilize her. I whispered in her ear, "You can do this. You got this, Em."

As I whispered, I glanced at Kristen's face. She had that wrinkled brow look of concern again, and this time, I understood what it meant.

She senses me.

Maybe Kirsten didn't know it was me she sensed, but she knew she felt something. I got the feeling she was going to protect her charge like a mama bear.

I was back to being elated again. My baby was in good hands.

As I helped Emily get through the therapy session, I felt like a man again, supporting my wife when it seemed like she wasn't going to make it. That afternoon, I made the most of every moment with Em, knowing full well it could be my last. There were brief times when I felt Em was aware I was with her. I could sense her love pulsating against my body. It was warm and wrapped my body like a second skin. At least I thought I could feel it.

When my energy began to sputter, I reluctantly transported back to the Outer Banks. It was a bittersweet moment. But at least now I knew that Emily was successfully on the road to recovery.

CHAPTER 25

The Second Almost Visit...

As it turned out, I needed to recharge for a long time before I could consider another visit with Emily. My trip had zapped all my energy and more. I didn't even have enough juice to transport to the Dune Burger for several days.

Luke, bless his heart, never said a word. But he did make it convenient for me to rest for a while. And in my absence, he had developed a power routine to help me charge up more rapidly. This time I took the process more seriously. I knew what the rewards were and I was determined to get even more significant ones.

I didn't know if I would ever reveal myself to Emily. To be honest, materializing in front of her scared me. I didn't know what would happen, but nothing was going to stop me from seeing Emily again.

So, when I was finally ready, I transported to Emily's hospital room in Maryland.

But someone else was laying in her bed.

Did I have the wrong room?

Unfortunately, I was once again fully charged again and visible. And this time, the occupant saw me.

"Who are you, young man? Have you come to carry me to Heaven?" An old man in bright blue pajamas asked me.

At first, I didn't know what to say.

I mean, what do you say to an old guy when you magically materialize out of thin air? I racked my mind looking for a reasonable explanation. There was none.

"No, I'm an angel, but I have lost my way. Please go about your business."

"No... wait... I haven't had a visitor in such a long time. Please sit with me awhile."

The man was begging me with his eyes. I couldn't say no.

"If you like, I could hang out with you for a bit. I'd like to make a new friend."

"Thank you... thank you." The man cried. His loneliness broke my heart.

I pulled a deck of cards from my pocket and asked, "Would you like to play a game of Old Maid?"

"I love Old Maid. My Frannie and I played the Old Maid card game when we were first married. We didn't have much money, but we did have a deck of cards. We played every Saturday night."

"I learned how to play a short while ago. By the way, my name is Jordan."

"A wonderful name. You can call me, George. Or Handsome. Whatever rocks your boat."

His comment made me laugh. Old George was a trip. It turned out he had been married 52 years to his wife when she died of cancer the year before. Their only child had been killed in the war, and all of their family and friends had either passed or were in hospice or elderly care homes, so he didn't get any visitors. The poor man was lonely.

All during my stay, I sat on the edge of his bed and played card games with him until it was time for him to go to sleep. As I was getting ready to leave, George asked me to visit again. I said yes. I liked the old guy.

CHAPTER 26

Let's Try This Again Visit…

Before attempting another visit, I quizzed Luke on things like how to stay invisible no matter how juiced you were and how to find out where Breathers were located, my Breather being Emily. I was determined to check in on her without her seeing me.

I know, I know, it was foolish, but I couldn't help it. I was still afraid she'd reject me. All those ghost romances people read are sweet and all that, but tell the truth… can you honestly say that you'd be happy to see a ghost, face to face? I was afraid Em couldn't handle it. I know she said she wanted to see me but I was dead. I was a different guy now. It wasn't the same. I wasn't the same.

Anyway, I also asked Luke if I could recharge during my visit. I know that sounds silly. I mean electricity is electricity, right? But what if I was violating some rule or something? Turns out, I was worrying about nothing. I just had to be extra careful that no other LDs caught me. Apparently, they are very turf possessive.

I tried to think of everything and anything that could happen while I was away so I'd be prepared. I was trying to be more independent. But, I was still such a newbie at the whole death thing that I couldn't think of everything, so I had to rely on Luke to help me more than I wanted. I have to admit Luke went above and beyond all expectations. It was good to have friends.

But I still had to deal with the worst nemesis of all – time. I didn't have a clue of how much time had flown by since I had died. After all, time didn't mean as much since I had become an LD. It seemed the longer I was LD, the less I could keep track of it. So at this point, I didn't have a clue as to where Emily was in her recovery and her life. I didn't even know where I might find her on a particular day so I was taking a shot in the dark in guessing as to where I should transport my butt. I figured I better cross my fingers, my toes, and whatever else I could cross before I tried to transport again.

Pray for me, please?

***

It must have been my lucky day because I chose the right place, right time. I went to Emily's parents' house and found her in the shower. Yup, it sure was my lucky day.

I stripped off my clothing (old living habit, I know) and slipped into the shower stall with her. At first, I stood there and let the water flow through me. Surprise… I had expected it to cascade down my body, much like when I was living. But no, it went through me.

I decided I had a duty to be of some help, so I helped Emily suds herself. There were all kinds of places she missed if you catch my drift. I'm pretty sure she felt my presence because her body relaxed as she hummed a familiar tune, one of my favorites. She always hummed when we showered together.

God, how I miss her humming.

Anyway, I continued to guide Emily's hand as she slid it the length of her thigh.

Ah, the good life.

When Emily got ready to shave her legs, I knelt in front of her. I wanted to be able to guide her fingers as she slid the razor across her skin. It was Heavenly, let me tell you. I stroked her calves and kissed the tender spot behind her knee that I had discovered on our honeymoon. Emily seemed to enjoy it. I know I did.

I had just watched her reach for her loofa when it dawned on me it had been many months, if not a year or two since my first visit. During that last visit, Emily had been in recovery from back surgery. No way could she have shaved her legs let alone take a shower by herself. I had missed a lot while I was off on my dead life adventure. I felt myself gasp at the realization.

What else was I going to miss?

Does she remember the tiny things we used to tease each other about?

How long before she forgets about me?

I drew back into myself and away from her. The pain of Emily possibly forgetting me made me want to melt into the shower walls.

My eyes avoided gazing at her face until I couldn't stand it anymore and looked. Emily must have felt me move away because sadness tugged at her lips, the twinkle evaporated from her eyes. I had hurt her again. I hated myself.

I stepped toward her again to comfort her. As I wrapped my arms around her, she leaned into me as she stood under the shower head. Maybe it was an illusion, but I believe she felt me again. I was convinced of it when she began to hum another verse of that same tune I knew so well.

I swear I would give anything if we could stay like that, entwined forever.

CHAPTER 27

A few days later, Luke and I were at The Black Pelican teaching Maggie and Elise how to play Go Fish. I won't lie, the ladies were more charming than usual, and Luke was showing his rakish side, playing little tricks on us. I should have been happy, but I couldn't get into it. My heart hurt too much.

"Do you have any threes?" Maggie asked, holding her cards tightly to her chest. Earlier she had accused Luke of cheating. He had denied the charge, but she wasn't taking any chances.

"No, go fish." My cards were in plain view, but no one looked.

I don't know what I wanted, but it wasn't this. Not now. No matter how much I loved being with my friends, I couldn't ignore my breaking heart. My mind mulled over my options. I couldn't go see Emily again. Not yet. I didn't know what I was going to do about her. But I had to see her again because she and I were one, right? I didn't know what I should do anymore.

And then it came to me. What I needed was a break from everything. From Emily, from the OBX, from all that was in my dead life. I needed to step away from everything that reminded me of the accident and all that I had lost. I needed a vacation from… being me.

It occurred to me a visit to see George might be the pick-me-up I needed. It would take my mind off of my insecurities with Emily and my frustration at being dead. It excited me like nothing had recently. I made up my mind to tell Luke about it after we left the Pelican later that night. Until then, I would play cards with my friends and try not to be too much of a downer.

Anyway, I don't know when exactly it happened, but when it came around to my turn, I had looked up to see a clear reflection of their cards in the window. I don't know why I looked, I just did.

What is wrong with me? That is cheating, plain and simple. I should tell them that I can see their cards.

"Anyone got any kings?" I asked, knowing full well Maggie and Elise both had one.

I was so mesmerized, staring at that reflection that I didn't notice that Maggie had caught me. Somehow, she knew in an instant that I had seen their cards. Her face flamed red as she gave me a sharp kick under the table.

"Ow! That hurts," I complained.

"We are moving this game to another table. One without windows or reflections, young man. I don't understand why you men feel a need to cheat. It's just a friendly game."

Maggie said some more choice words about me and my heritage, but I can't repeat that sort of language.

Luke hung his head. I knew he was innocent and that my… my screw-up was reflecting negatively on him. I spoke, trying my best to defend him and defuse the situation.

"I swear to you that I didn't purposely look at your cards, Maggie. It was just a fluky thing. I looked up, and there was the reflection. I know I shouldn't have looked but I did, and I'm sorry. Please, please forgive me. I swear it won't happen again. And please don't blame Luke. He doesn't cheat. He's a very honorable man."

Maggie just stared at me. Elise shot me a glance, shaking her head as I blushed. Even Edna Jean summoned up enough energy to wag her finger at me before disappearing. That hurt more than anything.

Good God, I was screwing up in all my relationships.

"Look, I know I haven't been much fun today. I've been sulky and thinking only of myself. And now you think I was cheating. I can't change what happened, I can't seem to do anything right today. I don't want to make things worse so I'll just go ahead and leave. I'll try to make it up to you later."

"No, you will not leave, sir. Not until you give us the fair game we wish to play." Maggie exclaimed with her arms folded across her chest and her toe tapping. Thank goodness her face wasn't flaming red anymore, but her lips were thin, white slashes. I knew she meant business.

Luke gave me a nudge with his elbow. I turned to look at him, and he shot me a look that said I better consider her request.

I knew Luke was right, so I stayed, and lost big time. At the end of the game, Maggie leaned in and tweaked my earlobe.

"Doesn't feel good, now does it?" Maggie asked. The tone of her voice stung me.

"Karma," I said.

"What did you say, sir?"

"Karma. It means I deserved what I got."

"Humph, yes you did, sir. Now give me a kiss and all will be forgotten." Maggie used her index finger to indicate where on her cheek I was to place said kiss.

I obliged because I was genuinely sorry. My face blazed crimson as the others smirked and jostled each other behind Maggie. I couldn't complain about the public shaming, I deserved every bit of it.

"Please, let me make it up to you, Maggie. Is there anything I can do to show you how sorry I am? So that you'll forgive Luke and me? I'll do anything. Your friendship means a lot to me," I said, hoping my sincerity was heard.

Maggie stared at me for a minute, her head cocked to one side. Well, at least her lips weren't slashes anymore.

"Pedicures. Once a week for a month. I know how much you enjoyed it the last time," Maggie said. I must have cringed because she continued, "for Elise and for me. Make it three months."

Well, I had received the worst punishment I could imagine. Hell had nothing over those horrible toes of Maggie.

"You got it. I hope you will be able to forgive me in time."

Whew, I was relieved. It could have been worse.

Maggie leaned in and kissed me on the cheek. "Oh, I forgive you. I forgave you the instant I saw you cheating because I know it's not in your heart to be a cad. I feel a moral obligation to ensure this dead life doesn't change you. Going to the dark side always starts with little indiscretions," she said, patting my hand. "Besides, Elise and I needed more pedicures."

That broke the ice. I loved Maggie's sense of humor. Now I knew that all was forgiven.

Once my punishment was settled, Maggie dealt the cards again. Elise and the others sat in their newly assigned seats, as did I. I won the next hand. I am sure that Maggie let me as a reminder that she was in charge.

I promise you that from that point on, I kept my eyes down. And whenever possible, I kept my back to the windows. I also thought about what Maggie said – that going to the dark side started with little indiscretions. I suppose I had become a bit complacent since dying. I didn't really give rules much thought anymore. I'd have to be more careful in my dead life if I wanted to stay a good guy.

And now, I had too much to think about so my visit with George would have to wait. I felt that if I tried to visit him some of the bad vibes from today would follow me. I would have to wait to attempt another visit when I had a more positive attitude.

CHAPTER 28

The next day, I gathered together a little bag of goodies for George. There were crossword puzzles, a few books, a paint-by-numbers kit, and a Kindle Fire reader loaded with books and movies. And no, I didn't shoplift. I am proud to say I am even better than Luke when it comes to finding loose change and valuables on the beach. I paid for everything.

Before heading off to visit George, I transported to the Dune Burger to check on Luke. I was a little worried because Luke had mentioned he was having some sort of trouble and I wanted to see if I could help in some way. But Luke wasn't there. So now I was even more concerned, but there was nothing I could do so I transported to George's room.

***

Visiting George...

The moment I popped into George's room, it was clear something was wrong. George didn't look right. His color was a pasty gray, and he was hooked up to several machines. The room smelled of... death.

Crap... Georgie's about to cross over.

I walked over and sat on the edge of George's bed. Placing the back of my hand on his forehead, I checked to see if I could feel his temperature. I don't know if I could or not, but he didn't feel hot to touch. So, I grabbed his chart at the foot of his bed and flipped through the pages. It didn't look promising. George might get better, but there was only a slim percentage of survival in his favor.

"George, are you awake?" I asked putting my hand on his.

As I rubbed the back of George's hand, he smiled at me with his eyes. Even with the gray cast on his skin, he looked 100% better.

"Hey, George. I came for a visit. Sorry, I took so long."

"I was beginning to think you'd weren't coming back, Jordan. Say, are those gifts in your bag for me?"

Well, it would appear there was nothing wrong with George's eyesight. Laughing, I handed him the bag. It was like watching a five-year-old at Christmas. To say he looked pleased was an understatement.

"I saw those and thought you'd like them," I said as George pulled one game after another from the bag.

I watched George examine one pinball game that featured Monster trucks.

"You remembered."

"I remember everything you said, George."

Next, George pulled an adult coloring book from the bag. He looked at me, his eyes bursting with questions.

"Apparently, that's a thing now. It's supposed to let you relax and be creative at the same time."

"And it's not for children?"

"No. See?" I pointed to the title where it said - adult. "There's some molding clay too. Now on that, if you make something, I'll have to find a way to get it fired for you and then you can paint it."

"Cool beans," George said.

Oh, George, you are so funny.

Then, he pulled the Kindle Fire from the bag, and the rest of the gifts were forgotten for the moment. Once I showed him all the bells and whistles, the Kindle became his favorite gift. He liked it so much that we had to watch a movie on it right away. The movie was an old Kevin Costner film, *Wyatt Earp*.

When the movie finished, I heard George sigh. Not a good sigh, more like a weary, giving-up sigh. I turned to look at him.

"Frannie and I saw *Wyatt Earp* when it first came out and loved it. I still love it. So much fun."

George was back to looking like a lump of gray paste. Just watching the movie had worn him out. That worried me.

"Maybe you better get some sleep. You have to rest if you want to get better." I put my hand on George's upper arm to reassure him.

He shook his head. "It won't do any good. I'm dying. We all know it. Even the nurses have been giving me extra pudding with dinner. And you know getting extra pudding is a sure sign they know you're going to kick the bucket." George raised an eyebrow as if to add emphasis.

I laughed harder than I should have. I guess my nerves got the better of me. You'd think a trained doctor would react better to this sort of situation. I never want anyone to die, but I had just begun to get to know George. It was too soon for him to leave. I decided to tell him about an idea I had.

"George, I want to talk to you about something. I usually hang out in North Carolina. Have you ever been to the OBX?"

"Once, when I was a kid my family went there on vacation."

"Well, when you get better I want you to come to the OBX. We could spend more time together, and it would be a good place for you to spend your… ummmm…"

"My final days on earth? Jordan, you can say it. I'm okay with it. When it's time for me to pass on, I'll get to see my Frannie again and the son we lost in the war. I can't wait to see my parents and brother again too."

"You're still young enough for a few more memories, George. I'd like you to come to the OBX. But you need to get better, or you won't be able to come."

George leaned back on his pillows. By the way his eyebrows were dancing on his forehead, I would have to say he was thinking things over.

"I'll come," George finally said.

"Great. Listen, you need to get some rest now, and I need to head back. I'll come to see you soon, and we'll make plans."

"Sure, Jordan. Please come closer, I'd like to hug you."

A real hug with a Breather wasn't possible for me. But I wanted to try, so I moved closer as George held his arms out. I got close enough that my cheek was against his. As I felt his arms pull together across my back, I could feel his heartbeat through his thin hospital gown, it was weak. Stabs of sorrow sliced through my own heart because I knew in that instant that my friend, George, had lied to me. He didn't want me to know that the end was nearer than his chart revealed. The doctors had been too generous in their diagnosis. Or maybe he was willing himself to die. No matter which it was, George wasn't long for this world.

George sighed and pulled away. Now George must have a very vivid imagination because I know he couldn't feel me but he sure thought he did. Maybe some hugs are solely in your head.

"I can now say I hugged an angel. I can check that off my bucket list."

As I pulled back, I saw George was smiling. He looked... satisfied with his decision.

"I might pop in tomorrow to see how you are," I said.

142

"I'll be here. I'm going to take that nap now if you don't mind." George closed his eyes.

I stood there for a moment, unable to let go. But the doctor in me felt the right thing would be to accept George's choice and so I did. I would come back tomorrow to say goodbye, even if we both continued to lie about the future.

As I got ready to transport back home, I looked at my friend's face one last time. I noticed a single tear on his cheek. I touched it, taking home a piece of George to the OBX.

CHAPTER 29

The next day, after I recharged myself, I transported to the Dune Burger, only to discover Luke had already gone off somewhere. So I transported to what was now, my second home, The Black Pelican. But the ladies were busy arguing over something again, and I couldn't handle any discord today. I just couldn't. Since the ladies hadn't seen me, I snapped my way out of that wasp's nest.

Back at the Dune Burger, I sat at one of the picnic tables and listened to the ocean waves, feeling sorry for myself. In my wallowing, I got the bright idea to go to see Allie. I wanted to ask her how Emily was. My guilt over hurting my wife was still intense, but I needed to be reassured Emily was all right.

***

Snap!

"Hey, you could give a girl some warning," Allie shouted.

I looked around. I was standing in a bathroom doorway.

Oops.

Allie, wearing baby-doll pajamas, was standing in front of the mirror over her sink. There was no one behind me or in the bathroom with her, so I guessed she was yelling at me. Looking at her more carefully, it dawned on me that she was in the middle of curling her hair with a curling iron.

Double oops.

"I'm so sorry. Should I come back later?" I asked her.

"No, I'm almost done. Why don't you go into my living room until I finish my hair and we'll chat in a minute, okay?"

I hung my head, embarrassed that once again, I had miscalculated my arrival spot. I practically ran from the room, not wanting to make another transporting miscalculation.

About thirty minutes later, Allie joined me. She had finished curling her hair and had put on makeup. She also had changed into a pair of jeans and a shirt. She walked over to her loveseat sofa and patted the cushion next to her to indicate where I was to sit.

"So, it seems you have learned a few tricks since I last saw you."

"I have a friend who's been teaching me the ropes of being dead."

"So you're adapting. That's great."

"I don't know how great it is. It's not like I have a choice."

"Sorry." Allie tried to touch my hand, but her hand slipped right through mine into the sofa seat. I have to give her credit. She didn't jerk her hand back. Instead, she inched her hand back onto the cushion between us.

"It's not something you need to feel sorry for. It is what it is."

"I'm sor… I mean okay. Can I help you in some way?"

"I went to see Emily in Maryland. She sensed me, but I couldn't um… stay." I couldn't look her in the eye as I practically admitted that I could have revealed myself to Emily but chose not to.

"Emily called me right after your visit. She was crying because you didn't let her see you."

I walked over and pretended to examine some trinkets on her hutch by the window. I had my back to Allie because I didn't want her to see my pain.

"I can't let her see me. It hurts too much."

Allie twisted in her seat to look at me as we spoke.

"What hurts? Tell me so I can help you. Please come and sit with me."

I went back to the sofa and sat… as far away as I could. The whole couch wasn't much bigger than the overstuffed chairs at my mother's house so I couldn't get very far away even if I wanted to.

"I know I should want her to live her life, but I'm struggling with the idea that I'll never get more."

Allie stared at me with penetrating eyes. We sat in silence for several minutes with her staring at me and me avoiding her eyes.

"You want to be with her in a relationship."

"Desperately." My voice broke as I spoke.

"Jordan, why didn't you go into the light? You know, when you died."

"I didn't see the light. One minute, I was trying to avoid an accident but ended up crashing the car anyway, and the next minute, I found myself outside the car, looking in at my body. But there were no lights anywhere except for my car's flickering headlights until they died too."

"You must know you were left here for a reason."

"I had to get help for Emily… so she didn't die too."

Allie put her hand on mine… well, she hovered it over mine.

"It's bigger than saving Emily. I think you stayed behind because there is something more you are supposed to do."

I bit my lip, giving me a moment to think. Allie patiently waited.

"Luke… he's an angel I met… he says the same thing. Okay, I get that, but I want to know why a relationship with Emily isn't possible. Can't I do both?" I lifted my eyes to gaze into Allie's. I was desperate for her to tell me I could.

"Sweetie, I am so sorry, but the dead are dead. A final goodbye is what both of you need and should have, but anything else will keep Emily from moving on. I know it hurts you to realize that Emily will eventually want to meet someone new."

I jumped to my feet, and with a burst of fury, I didn't know I had in me, I destroyed everything on Allie's coffee table.

Sweeping the fragile glass pieces onto the floor with my fist, I shouted, "No!" as loud as I could. I was so loud I could hear the glass cracking in Allie's bay window.

The sound of the glass cracking brought me back to my senses. I looked from the window to Allie's face which was now white with red splotches. Her tiny fists were grabbing on the couch pillow like it was a safety net. I had terrified her.

Why? Why can't I have a conversation without hurting people?

"I have to go. I'm sorry."

I left before she could say a word.

I hated myself.

I hated my existence.

I even hated God at that moment.

CHAPTER 30

After coming back from Allie's, I hid in my closet at the hospital for a long time. Curled up in the corner, I was too busy mentally beating myself up to notice the world around me. I think Luke came to check up on me a few times, but he didn't speak and left before I could even open my eyes. I didn't go looking for him because all I wanted to do was crawl away from my pain.

I wallowed in my misery until I felt nothing.

Eventually, my energy was nearly gone. I was so low I couldn't transport, so I got on the old skateboard Luke had given me and skated to a store closed for the night. Inside I found an open outlet and gave myself a power boost. It took a long time to fill myself again but eventually, I returned to my ghostly self.

As I left the store, I noticed an old man shuffling along the street toward me. He was walking a dog. As they got closer, the dog saw me even though his human didn't. The dog warned me with a low growl,

I was to stay away from his human, I suppose. When I didn't high tail it out of there, he pulled at his collar with a frenzy of yapping.

The old man called to him, "George… George, calm down. There's nothing there. Settle down, boy."

George… my God, I had forgotten to visit him. He must hate me by now like everyone else I had let down.

I wasn't going to wait anymore. I transported myself to George's room.

CHAPTER 31

A Last Visit with George...

I was in luck. George was still hanging on.

My friend must have sensed me when I popped in because his eyes opened immediately.

"You came back." George held out his arms to me for a hug. I didn't want to disappoint him, so I ghost-hugged him. His heartbeat sounded so feeble, I was worried it might stop at any minute.

"Frannie's been by to see me. Twice. I told her I couldn't go until I said goodbye to my friend."

"Frannie? Are you sure it was Frannie and not one of the nurses or doctors?" I was confused.

When someone went into the light, they couldn't come back unless they came back to guide a loved one into Heaven, right?

I scratched my head. For the life of me, I couldn't grasp what he was saying. I felt my face scrunch up and then my mind cleared.

Wait… she's come for George.

George patted my hand, so to speak. "I wanted to tell you I appreciate you being my friend. And I'll miss you, but I suspect you have other people who need your help."

"Are you sure you want to go? You haven't come to the OBX yet."

"I'm sure. I will miss getting to see your OBX wonderland, but I'm going to the real paradise. I miss my Frannie, and I need her. You understand, right?"

How could I not understand? Emily is my soul.

"Jordan, I know something else."

My heart skipped a beat. What could Geoge possibly be talking about?

"I know you are not an angel. Not yet anyway. You probably just didn't want to hurt an old man's feelings on that night you first popped in here. I understand. But you can make it up to me. Before it's time for me to go, I'd like to hear about your wife. She's still alive, isn't she?"

I followed his eyes. He was looking at my wedding ring. Sighing, I nodded.

For the next few hours, we talked about how Emily and I met in the third grade. And how we almost missed our perfect wedding. He laughed when I told him we had gotten locked in a Kohl's store the night before our ceremony because Em and I fell asleep in a hammock we were trying out before buying for our new house. I told him about everything from the wedding to the night she announced we were expecting, all the way up to our last vacation. And then we talked about the accident that had torn us apart. I enjoyed our conversation, it was nice sharing my memories of Em with a friend like George. It was almost like when I was alive.

"I'm sorry you're stuck here. I hope you don't think you have to be Emily's angel until it's her time to go. I know I wouldn't like that. After all, eventually, a healthy woman wants a family, and your Emily will be no different. It would be hard to have to watch her moving on."

This time I didn't go into a rage. I was willing to accept life was going to go on without me. And no, I didn't want to watch Emily with anyone else but if my purpose was to be her guardian angel so be it.

"I'll do whatever needs to be done to protect Emily." I crossed my arms to keep myself calm.

"I hope I didn't hurt you," George said with his eyes on my arms.

"I know you want the best for me."

"I hope you get to be with Emily and your son in Heaven one day," George said in a worn voice. I wondered if he would last the night.

"So, shall we watch one more movie together?"

George grinned. "I did see one on my Firebug thingy that looked interesting."

I burst out laughing.

How can you not laugh when a sweet man like George says something funny?

"Why are you laughing, Jordan?"

"The Firebug name makes me laugh, it just sounds funny. So what movie are we watching on the Firebug?"

"*Guardians of the Galaxy*. I overheard the nurses talking about it. Apparently, the one actor is hunkilicious."

Now, I couldn't stop laughing. I was going to miss George. Big time.

"Oh, and I thought that I'd leave the Firebug and those games and things for the children's ward here. Do you mind?" George asked.

"That's a great idea, George. It would make me very happy."

***

And so we watched *Guardians of the Galaxy* on the Firebug. The nurses were right, that actor was hunkilicious. We no sooner finished the movie when this bright light burst into the room. It was so luminous I had to shield my eyes.

George whispered, "It's time. Do you see my Frannie? Isn't she lovely?"

I turned my eyes toward where George was looking and saw a beautiful woman in her thirties float out of the light and over to George. She wrapped her arms around George's neck and kissed inch after inch of his face.

I was about to tell George he was a dog to be married to such a young girl when I remembered something my grandmother used to say. At the time, it didn't make any sense, but now it did. Everyone in

Heaven is thirty, the perfect age. At thirty, we are fully formed and have not yet developed those aches and pains that age brings on. At thirty, we are youthful and at the prime of our lives.

The machines monitoring George began to make a racket with their bells and dinging. My pulse quickened as I cheered for George to get away with his Frannie before the doctors and nurses rushed into the room to perform heroic feats to save his life. If I hadn't been so caught up in the moment, I would have figured out a way to pull the plugs myself, but I didn't want to miss a moment of George and Frannie's reunion.

I watched George's soul rise from his body and float next to his Frannie. When they embraced, I saw George whisper something to her. They turned in my direction and waved, Frannie blew me a kiss and George winked as he became thirty again. They made such a beautiful couple.

The whole experience was so joyful. I could almost hear the angels singing, and the bells of Heaven ringing as a second even more luminous white light filled every crevice in the room. I knew that the light was a Heavenly spirit, surrounding George and Frannie to take them home.

When I sensed the spirit gazing upon me, a warmth I can't explain enveloped me. I felt safe from all harm. And then the spirit filled me with the thought that I would be accepted into Heaven one day but not yet.

A moment later the light withdrew from the room, and the spirit of George was gone. His body was still in his bed, frail, broken, and no longer of use to anyone. I was sad, but I was also joyous. It was a moment of hope for me. One day that would be Em and me, I just knew it.

When the nurses and doctors came running into the room, I transported back home.

There was nothing left for me there.

CHAPTER 32

When I transported back to the OBX, I was a changed man. The ladies of The Black Pelican noticed right away. No one said a word, but each of them hugged me as if I needed it. Even Luke didn't tease or play his practical jokes for the first few days. No one asked me what had happened, but I suspected they knew anyway. After all, Luke had told me some time ago that ghosts gossip.

"I need to tell you something, but I don't want you to do anything stupid," Luke said as he shuffled the playing cards.

"Me do something stupid? Nah." I winked at Maggie.

Elise walked in at that moment. She had been downstairs nagging the chef again. It was funny to me that Elise cared so much about what the chef was preparing for Breathers. But apparently, she considered herself a gourmet cook and couldn't help herself.

"What did I miss?" Elise asked.

"Nothing," everyone spoke at once. Out of the corner of my eye, I saw Maggie miming the 'zip your lips' motion in Elise's direction.

Uh oh, what's up now?

"Well, I guess you all need new faces because Jordan looks curious, Luke looks nervous, and you Maggie, you look on edge. Is this about Jordan's Emily being here last night?" Elise said as she sat across from me.

"What?" I know I gasped, more than spoke the word.

It could not have hurt more if she had physically punched me in the chest.

"Now, now, we're not sure it was her. Yes, the young woman looked somewhat similar to the photo you showed us, but surely it was someone else," Maggie said. She put her hand on my arm, on my upper arm. The place where everyone touches you to show sympathy. She was lying.

"Was she alone?"

Just tell me and stop with all the toning things down crap.

"She was with a young lady. They had dinner and left. We didn't even notice them until they were getting ready to leave," Elise said.

I stood up and began to pace behind my chair. A million thoughts were running through my head.

Should I stay away from the Pelican in case she came back? When did she move to the OBX? Or was she here for a visit and would be returning to Annapolis shortly? Would she be here again tonight? Maybe she was downstairs right now.

"Hold on there, bucko. You're a changed dude, remember?" Luke put in his two cents.

I didn't speak out loud, did I?

"You're right, but I still love her. And I still want to see her, but I need to be calm about it. I'll be cool." I leaned back in my chair. "See? I can control myself. So you saw Emily, did she look happy?"

Elise and Maggie exchanged looks.

"She looked content, but I wouldn't say joyous," Maggie offered.

"Definitely not joyous," Elise chimed in.

"You should leave it alone for now," Luke said.

"Leave it alone? Why? She's my wife."

"Emily was your wife. Now she's your widow. She has a right to get on with living."

I know my face flamed red. I couldn't do anything about that, but I could try to control my voice.

"You're right. I have no intentions of materializing in front of Emily. But I still want to see her."

No one spoke for a while. Instead, we stared at the cards in our hands as if we were about to make power moves.

"I'm surprised Em's back in town. Do any of you know where she's staying?"

Elise piped in first.

Good girl.

"When your Emily was enjoying her dessert, I overheard her and the other young lady talking about the house they are renting in Kill Devil Hills. She didn't mention which house, only that it's oceanfront."

"Thank you, Elise. By any chance did you catch the other woman's name?"

Before the others could stop her, "Allie," slipped out. Maggie got a hand on her, and when Elise turned her way, she signaled her to hush.

"Good. I like Allie," I said as I looked from face to face. "Look, I know I have no right to interfere in Emily's life, but I'm glad you told me she was in town. It would have been worse if I happened upon her one night. Now can we get back to the game? I feel like kicking some butt."

The ladies weren't sure what I was saying at first, but thankfully, Luke rose to take the bait. "Oh, it's on, Doc. It's on."

"Yes, I will kick behind too." Elise giggled.

"As will I, sir," Maggie piped in.

"You are a bad influence on the ladies, Doc." Luke teased.

I must say I did a good acting job for the duration of the evening. I played cards, made jokes, shared in some gossip, and no one was the wiser that I was dying to go downstairs in case Emily came in.

I swear I felt Edna Jean put her head on my shoulder to comfort me. But then again, you never know with shadow people.

CHAPTER 33

"You know I'm going to have to get even after this, right?" I shouted over the roar of the ocean waves.

I was clinging precariously to a boogie board Luke had convinced me to try. I didn't like it, not one bit. But he had told me he had a surprise for me if I at least made an attempt to try it.

"Come on, Dude. It's fun. We can test waves all along the coast together once you get the hang of it."

"No, way. This is like trying to walk on butter. Crap!"

A massive wave I didn't see in time swelled and knocked me off the board. I came sputtering to the surface.

Well, okay. The swell wasn't much at all, and the water barely came up to my thighs, but hey, I could have... I could have hurt somebody if my board got loose. It was apparent Luke thought it was a barrel of laughs to see me careening off into the water. He cackled behind his hands as I shook my trunks to get the sand out.

"Get back on, and I'll tell you a secret." Luke pointed to the board.

I pulled myself up on my board again and tried to balance myself as I attempted to get to my knees. I was thinking I might try surfing on my knees. It seemed a more stable approach for me.

Criminy, don't let him ask me to stand on the thing.

"I was thinking about your situation and wanted to ask you a question. If you were able to have a last night with Emily, could you let her go? I mean a physical, touchy-feely, kissy kind of night."

I turned to look at him, forgetting that a wave might hit at any moment.

"Is that even an option?"

"It would be dangerous for you, but yes, I believe it is. However, you shouldn't take the risk unless you are willing to let Emily go afterward."

"I could physically touch her, and she could touch me?" I paddled my board over to be alongside his. I wanted to look him in the eyes as we talked.

"Yup."

"So it would be the goodbye we never got?"

"Exactly. But it has to be a one-time thing. And you have to understand that if it goes wrong, you'll become a shadow person and maybe be stuck on earth for centuries."

"Unless I can say goodbye, I'm almost a shadow person anyway."

Luke stared at the shoreline.

"If we do this, you can still look in on her from time to time, but you have to promise you won't try to do this on your own again. It's one and done, understand?"

"Totally."

My heart jumped out of my chest and did a dance on my boogie board.

"You have to say the words."

"All right, I agree that it will be a one-time thing. If I have this one last night with her, I can never be with Emily again. Are you happy?"

"Tots, Dude. Now all you have to do is catch me." Luke laid on the board and paddled out to deeper waters.

"What?"

"Don't pretend you didn't hear me," Luke shouted over his shoulder.

I fell off my board just thinking about trying to ride a wave. Every wave looked like a monster wave to me so I tried to talk to myself in my head. I told myself I could do it. I told myself I was a winner. I told myself everything I could think of that would get up on that board.

I guess my pep talk jazzed me up because I scrambled onto the board on my stomach. The effort winded me, so I had to rest a second before I paddled after Luke. When I finally caught up with him, he grinned and gestured behind him.

Holy crap, here I go.

"See that wave? We're going to ride it to shore," he yelled over the sounds of the ocean.

I looked where Luke pointed. What I saw froze my heart in mid-beat.

Holy crap. That wave was charging toward us.

"Turn your board around and do what I do," Luke shouted.

And that was how I learned how to surf. It wasn't much different than not being able to swim and having your big brother throw you in the deep end of the pool.

But… I loved it!

The first wave threw me off halfway to shore, but I climbed back on and got better with each try. By the end of the afternoon, I was able to hang on and just about get to land without drowning or whatever they call it in the dead life.

***

When we got done surfing, we paddled to shore where we rolled off our boards and pulled them behind us. When we reached the sandy beach, Luke put his arm around me as we walked.

"I'm proud of you, little one," Luke said.

"I'm proud of me too."

"So a deal's a deal. Later tonight I'll tell you about my idea." Luke said as he washed the sand off his board in the surf and put it under one arm.

Wow, I had forgotten entirely about his idea for helping me have a last goodbye with Emily.

"You know maybe we'll sit on the last night idea for a few days. I want to perfect this surfing thing first."

Luke gave me a sideways glance. I knew he was thinking I had gone back to being fearful of showing myself to Emily. He was right. I was terrified.

CHAPTER 34

Later On...

Luke and I took some magazines and nail glitter to Maggie and Elise. The girls had mentioned the glitter the last time I saw them, and I didn't see the problem with them having a little glitz in their lives. But Luke had chastised me for bringing them into my century. He said he liked them being quaint. So I presented him with the argument that they were women, and women were attracted to shiny things no matter when they were born. He couldn't argue with me, so I gave him a few bottles of polish for him to give to the girls.

When we were ready, we transported together.

***

"You are late," Maggie wagged her finger in my face while Elise paced behind her, wringing a handkerchief between her hands.

"What's wrong?" I asked, looking at Luke. Elise was whispering something to him. He looked away as if he didn't want to be a part of this conversation.

"Emily is here," Maggie cried out.

Meanwhile, Elise shook her head, no, no, no. This didn't sound good at all.

Crap, there goes those cold fingers grabbing my heart again.

"Em? Is she with Allie?"

"Noooooooo. Miss Emily's with a man," Elise's voice burst like a popping balloon. "What are we going to do?"

A knife went straight through my heart. For a second, I considered leaving.

I can't see another man with my Emily.

But Maggie had some other ideas on the subject. She grabbed me by my hand and dragged me downstairs to the dining area.

***

And there she was.

Em looked great. She was tan, and her hair fell down her back in shiny curls. Em always had silky hair. My favorite thing in the world was to brush it as she sat on the floor between my legs. And she had on my favorite outfit. I wished I could take a photo of how perfect she looked.

"There he is. What are you going to do about it?" Maggie pointed at a man who sat opposite Emily.

I took a couple of steps to get a better view of the man. It was only when he turned to gaze across the room that I got a good look at his face.

Emily was having dinner with her cousin, Bobby Parker. The three of us used to pal together in grade school until his parents moved out of state.

When I laughed with relief, Maggie grabbed my arm. "What's so funny? You should be furious," she said.

"Furious," Elise added.

"I'm laughing with relief, Maggie. That guy's name is Bobby. He's Emily's cousin, and not the kissing kind," I chortled.

Geez, my relief is making me sound crazy.

"Cousin?" Both women asked at once.

Luke slapped me on the back and said, "Sure am glad that bullet was dodged."

The four of us watched Emily and Bobby talk for a few minutes. It was like old times for me.

Suddenly, Maggie gasped. We all turned to see what was wrong. She pointed across the room.

T.L. had entered through the doorway from the kitchen. The rage of his face practically set his goatee on fire. Before we could stop T.L., he marched across the room, right up to Bobby's side. He looked from Emily to Bobby and back, his fists clenched at his side. Suddenly, T.L. did the unexpected. He levitated Bobby's dinner plate and dumped it on his head.

Well, the entire dining room went crazy. It was my birthday party all over again. People whipped out their phones and took photos of everything and anything. I guess they were hoping to catch those weird orbs ghost hunters claim are ghosts. Several diners pointed out spirits they insisted they saw. Not one of them pointed at us. Not fingers or cameras.

Over in the corner, Maggie and Elise had frozen looks of fear on their faces. And smart ass Luke was having a ball. He moved glasses on tables, levitated silverware. You name it, Luke did it.

Then T.L. marched over to me and got in my face.

"Sir, are you going to defend your woman's honor or must I do it for you?" T.L. demanded to know, with spit punctuating every word.

I ducked to avoid getting hit by a wadded napkin Luke had thrown. I don't know why I dipped. Logically, I knew the thing would have gone through me, but I moved out of the way anyway. When I stood up, T.L. was about an inch from my face.

"T.L. there's been a mistake. That man is my wife's cousin. She's not on a date or outing with another man."

A flash of confusion passed over T.L.'s face "Sir, the cad speaks to her like a loved one."

"They have always been close." I touched his upper arm. "Thank you for looking out for me."

Meanwhile, the dining room was evolving into near brawl status.

T.L. shook my hand. First time ever. I was not going to turn it down.

"I will take my leave, sir. It would appear you have everything in hand." And T.L. disappeared.

I looked around. Maggie and Elise were cowering on a chair in the corner of the dining room with their arms wrapped around each other. Luke had finally tired of his practical jokes. He was laying on the floor, on his side, watching the chaos. And the restaurant staff was attempting to calm the guests.

Over at Emily's table, she was pulling food from Bobby's hair. And Bobby was laughing like a hyena.

When Luke finally decided to join me, I said, "Let's take the girls upstairs."

***

It took a little cajoling to calm the girls down. Elise was hyperventilating from the fear of someone possibly discovering her. But once I told her that not one of the people downstairs had seen us, she calmed down. Maggie, on the other hand, was practically catatonic. It took her a bit longer. Funny, I would have thought Elise would have been the one who was more fragile.

Once we were all back to ourselves, we spent the rest of the evening playing cards and reliving what had happened downstairs.

"I misjudged T.L.," Luke admitted.

"I told you those stories couldn't be true."

Elise leaned over and whispered in Maggie's ear. Luke sorted his cards and casually said, "Looks like someone else thinks he's a good guy too."

"Sir, we were discussing the chaos that occurred downstairs." Maggie's face flamed crimson, her body stiff with indignation.

"Okay," Luke said through smirking lips.

"Let's get back to our game. Elise, do you have any threes?"

And so we got on with the rest of the evening.

CHAPTER 35

After I returned to my closet home, I sat in the corner in a beanbag chair I had brought in from a store in Nags Head. Over and over, I ran over my dilemma with Emily in my mind. It was a conversation I could only have with myself.

Wasn't I thrilled to be able to have one last night with Emily? Wasn't my perfect dream to be able to look into her eyes and run my fingers along her silky arms? Didn't we deserve a final kiss?

Well, before I became a living dead guy, it had been my dream. Now, I feared what I might see in her eyes. Would she recoil at my touch? I worried about taking the chance to find out.

I was slowly becoming a coward about my love.

***

"Take a seat," Luke said.

We were at the Pelican because it was raining outside and the thunder was loud. Not that rain affects us all that much, but it does make being outdoors less interesting.

The girls left us alone, apparently at Luke's request. *What was he up to?*

"Are we having a secret agent meeting?" I asked.

"I thought you were anxious to have one last night with Emily," Luke said as he fiddled with one of those spinner fidget things.

"I am. I thought I'd... I'd wait awhile." I began to examine my cuticles.

"What are you afraid of?" Good golly, he could spin that thing like nobody's business. Out of the corner of my eye, I could see it whizzing between his fingers.

"You're reading me wrong." I wondered how long I was going to have to scrutinize the skin around my nails.

"Right. You're afraid you'll disappoint Emily. Well, guess what, Doc.... You're wrong. It will be bittersweet, but you'll get the closure you both need."

"What if the sight of me makes her sick?"

My stomach started to punch it out with my heart. The first one to explode would win.

"You know for a college-educated boy, you sure are dumb. There is no doubt that she'll want to see you. Exactly as you are. Look, I know this whole dead thing is crappy but everyone dies sometime, and not many of us get a chance at a last goodbye."

"Maybe a last goodbye is at the heart of what I fear. It was tough enough to lose Emily the first time. The second might kill me except I'm already dead." I tried to make a joke, but it sounded so lame. I was surprised to hear Luke laugh.

He leaned in and patted me on the cheek.

"Don't waste a precious minute, Doc."

"So we're doing this?"

"We're doing this, Dude."

"Holy cow." My hands shook as I ran my fingers through my hair. "What do I need to do?"

"Meet with Emily's friend. Let her know what you are planning. Tell her to wait to tell Emily until an hour before you plan to arrive in case something goes wrong. I need at least three weeks to get you ready so let's try for a month from now."

"A month, okay. If I leave now, I can still catch Allie in her car before she leaves for home."

"Remember, tell her it's a one-time thing. We can't risk your safety trying it again."

Impulsively, I leaned forward and hugged Luke as tightly as I could. Then I stepped back and transported myself to Allie's car. As it turned out, Allie was excited. I had to remind her three times to keep it secret until an hour before my scheduled arrival.

CHAPTER 36

Getting ready for my night with Elise was comparable to training for the Olympics. I had to power binge every day for three weeks. In between sucking on electricity, I practiced appearing full body to people all over Nags Head.

At first, I would pop in some store like Gray's. I'd walk up to shoppers and say something to get a conversation going. There was no doubt they saw me the same as they saw the cashier or any other Breather. I was thrilled beyond belief. I had to keep reminding myself it was a temporary thing, revealing myself that is. When I looked like that, it was hard to remember that I was still dead.

We started out with brief periods, ten minutes here, and fifteen minutes there. Every day we extended it a few more minutes. By the twenty day mark, I was able to materialize in full body for close to four hours.

Next, it came time to test my feel factor. If my night with Emily was to be successful, the sense of touch had to be there for both of us. We selected Walmart in Kitty Hawk to launch that test.

First, I purposely bumped into one lady with a baby in her shopping cart and another toddler tied to her wrist by a leather harness. Unfortunately for me, the woman didn't have a pinhead of compassion.

"Oops, I am so—" I brushed against her as I tried to pass.

Well, the woman was a beast. As if I were nothing but a piece of fuzz on her finger, she shoved me with one hand, and I went flying. Let me tell you, her hand on my chest hurt. Big time. The woman had surprisingly bony fingers for a plump person.

Luke, of course, was beside himself, laughing his butt off again. But the first test resulted in a big fat pass. I was ready to try test number two.

Next, I reached for an item at the same time as a woman who could be the same age as my mother. And it was just my luck that she got the impression I was flirting with her. But I could feel her fingers wiggle under my own. They were warm and well… meaty.

I tried a few more times throughout the store until the best thing possible happened.

I got thrown out for harassing the shoppers.

Of course, Luke was watching and roaring with laughter.

Great, now he's going to remind me of this little tour into bizarro land, time and time again over our undead existence.

But it was all good because now I was ready for my night with Emily. To celebrate, we went to The Black Pelican and hung out with the ladies.

CHAPTER 37

"Jordan, would you do me a favor?" Maggie asked and then lowered her eyes to the ground.

Let me tell you those few words make me squirm. Usually, questions like that meant I was going to be asked to do something I in no way wanted to do. Even when I was alive, it seemed like I was the one guy who got suckered into some weird stuff and about half the time the other person would lead off with 'will you do me a favor?'

"I'm not going to have to repaint your toes, am I?"

Elise was way over in the corner of the room, showing Luke some piece of jewelry a diner downstairs had lost. I'm guessing she heard Maggie say the toe word because she yelled out, "Mine too, please."

I turned to Maggie, my eyebrows raised. Although their toes wouldn't be so bad this time since I had done them two weeks ago, I still wasn't ready to whip out the polish again.

"Oh goodness no. Since you have a medical background, I wanted to know if you'd pierce my bellybutton for me."

177

"Um, what?"

"I saw a young lady with hers done the other day and… I must say it looked awesome to me." Maggie giggled behind her hand.

"Did you just say awesome? Do you even know what that means?"

"Most certainly I know what it means, sir. I do watch those shows on that box downstairs. Now, I ask you again, will you do this for me?"

I sat in a chair and ran my hand through my hair, stalling until I could come up with a good excuse not to accommodate her. Possible infection wouldn't work, she was already dead. Neither would claiming it was too personal work because I was a doctor after all. Meanwhile, Maggie hovered at my shoulder.

Ooooh, I've got it.

"You don't want a piercing. It's pretty painful, Maggs," I advised.

"If you don't want to help me, just say so. And don't call me Maggs." Maggie's voice dripped with disappointment. The corners of her mouth turned down. I couldn't stand it.

"I'll do it." I gave in with an eye roll.

Maggie squealed with delight. Throwing her arms around my shoulders, she kissed me on my cheek.

I think I just got played. My girl, Maggie, recovered awfully quickly.

"Can you get me a nice belly button ring or better still, one of those dangly, sparkly diamond looking things?"

"I'll check into it. I need to find a piercing gun somewhere, too."

Maggie hurried off to huddle with Elise.

"But it will have to wait until after my visit with Emily," I called out after her, but Maggie didn't hear me. She and Elise were too busy giggling and whispering. I could tell by the way they kept looking at me I'd be piercing two belly buttons.

Holy moly, I sure hope their belly buttons aren't as gross as their toes.

A prickling on the back of my neck made me twist around to see what was causing it. I found T.L. standing behind me. He looked like he had something he was determined to say.

"Why don't you take a seat? We could chat for a few minutes before I leave," I said.

To my surprise, T.L. came around to face me. He held out his hand. I shook it, and he sat across from me.

"You seem to be a reasonably charitable chap," T.L. growled.

Was that a compliment?

"Thank you… Are you talking about the ladies?"

"Who else would I be talking about, sir?"

"Forgive me. I didn't mean to question you. When it comes to the ladies, I'm merely doing what one friend does for another. And I enjoy making them happy." T.L. was turning out to be a prickly guy to talk to. It made me wonder if he would ever change. "Is there something I could do for you?"

T.L. jutted out his chin and glared at the wall for a moment.

"I cannot leave this place," he waved his hand around as if to show me what he meant. "Therefore, I've never seen my wife's grave, and I would like to do so. Is there a way for you to help me?"

I didn't know if I was allowed to take T.L. out of the Pelican, so I offered something else.

"Would a photo satisfy your curiosity?"

T.L. turned to face me. His eyebrows were crinkled into matching question marks.

"A photograph? You have one of those magical boxes?"

"Something like that. I could get you a photo to keep. So you know where your wife is buried?"

"On Ocracoke. In a small cemetery behind the house where we lived."

"I will do my best."

The look on his face surprised me. His eyes shone brightly as if he were refusing to let a single tear escape. The skin under his left eye twitched. And best of all, it looked as if he were attempting a small smile.

"Let me ask you something. If I could get you a day trip out of here… and I'm not sure at all if it is possible, but I can look into it… would you like to see it in person?" I felt that as one human being to another, I would do my damnedest to get him to see his wife's last resting place.

Well, T.L. jumped to his feet and towered over me. He leaned over and dragging me to my feet, he tried to hug me, but it seemed like he didn't know where to put his hands or maybe didn't like the physicality of touching another man. So he slapped me on my back as if to punctuate the hug.

"Sir, you have treated me like I was your equal. Thank you. Thank you, sir. I won't forget this."

Immediately after saying his piece, he disappeared. I guess T.L. could only take so much goodwill at one sitting.

A split second later I realized that T.L. might have the idea that I promised I would take him out of the Pelican on a day trip.

"I'll try, but I can't make any promises," I shouted out to the walls.

The others turned to look at me. Sure, Luke was convinced my brains were fried from my training and sucking so much electricity. But the girls surprised me. They looked at me as if they had a bet going on as to when I would crack.

So I waved at them to set their minds at ease. And I made up my mind that I was going to demand Luke give me an honest answer on how I could get T.L. a day pass to see his wife's grave.

It was then that I felt the buzzing near my ear.

Well, hello Edna Jean.

I muttered as quietly as I could, "I haven't forgotten you, Edna Jean. I'm going to try to help you. Just give me a little more time."

I felt something on my cheek just as the buzzing stopped. I swear it felt like a kiss.

Having said my goodbyes… none of us was sure I would survive my little adventure… I was just about ready to go but first I needed was one more charge, so Luke and I were going to go to a new spot we found. It was another empty house so we'd have the place to ourselves as I topped off. Luke was walking toward me when a loud boom shocked all of us. It was quickly followed by sharp crackling noises as the lights went out.

The girls squealed with fear. Luke ran to the window and put his head through it. For a silly second, I forgot we were ghosts and didn't have to worry about things like opening and closing doors and windows. Anyway, he stuck his head outside. When he pulled himself back inside, he was cursing up a storm.

"Damn power surge. It looks like all of OBX is out."

"Out? You mean of electricity? No way. Not now of all times. I've got to have my last power boost."

Now I was worried… no, I was screwed.

"Come on, let's check around and see if we can find a house or business that still has electricity." Luke put his hand on my shoulder and snap!

***

In our search, we popped into one house after another with no luck. After that, we checked all the stores. No luck at all, not even the ones that should have had generators. Eventually, we were forced to admit defeat in the face of a historical event that had taken place and affected all of the OBX.

We could have taken some from the police station or hospital, but somehow that seemed like a bad idea considering they needed every bit of energy they had. And we felt leaving the OBX was not an option, the risk of getting stranded was too significant and time was running out for me.

There would have to be another way. Luke and I went back to The Black Pelican to consult with the girls in case they could suggest new places to look.

***

Back at the Pelican...

We all sat around a table, or rather Luke and the girls sat at the table. I walked in circles in the background. In two hours, Emily was going to be waiting for me, and I was going to have to be a no-show. Literally, because I wouldn't have that last power boost to be able to materialize and my sense of touch would be non-existent.

I know I was mumbling to myself and being of no use to the others, but I had lost my mind. I felt my chance at a last kiss was gone. Fate was having a great time destroying my life.

Having never been out of the Pelican in the last century, Maggie and Elise weren't much help. The best they could do was suggest areas.

"Did you check Manteo?" Elise asked.

"How about the Bodie Island Lighthouse? They have to keep it powered, don't they?"

"Checked both. Shoot, we even checked the Walmart in Kitty Hawk. Their backup generators got flooded," Luke said.

"Carova," Elise offered.

"Checked it. And nope," I said. I had personally checked Carova.

Meanwhile, outside it was pouring rain. A hurricane of epic proportions was headed toward us. No way would any crews get the power restored anytime soon. Even the streets were flooded by now.

Out of nowhere, a voice pulled me out of my funk.

"There's a power generator in the basement, sir. You could get your boost and then some," T.L. sounded like he was an expert. He had been standing in the corner apparently, taking in the discussion.

"How do you know what a power generator is?" I was astounded.

"Sir, a wise man adapts to his surroundings. The staff here, leaves the instructions for every power tool, television, electrical machine, whatever, lying wherever they drop it. I put my time to good use." T.L. sounded like he was bragging.

"Thank you, T.L. You may have saved my visit with Emily." I turned to the others. "Everyone, we're going to the basement."

Luke saved us the trip. He gathered everyone together and had us all touching him while he snapped his fingers. Instantly, we were all standing in front of the generator. Maggie and Elise were looking at Luke like he was a god.

Luke and T.L. got to working on getting the generator gassed up while I went upstairs to the dining area to make sure the restaurant was empty. We didn't need anyone coming down to check for burglars.

After we got the generator going, we circled around it. Maggie and Elise held hands and began praying. T.L. stood at my side while Luke plugged it in and stuck some straws in the outlet. He turned to me.

"You'll have to test it the hard way."

"Just like that." I think my concern was showing.

I didn't like the looks of the thing.

"Yup, just like that," Luke said impatiently.

"What if something goes wrong?" I had to ask. "I don't want to become a shadow guy."

Luke looked around and grabbed a wooden chair.

"If it goes south, I'll hit you with the chair and break the contact."

Would that even work on a dead guy like me?

"Oh, for the sake of all that is mighty, will you please suck it?" T.L. demanded.

And so I did. It was a weird power boost, to say the least. Not all power generators give the same output of electricity. This one was sporadic. I suppose you wouldn't notice if you were using it to keep your heat going or refrigerator running but using it the way I had to? Well, let's just say I wasn't the only one sucking.

But I didn't have to suck long before it ran out of gas. My special night was going to hell in a hand basket. I wouldn't be able to appear full body to Emily.

"Can we get some more gas for it?" Maggie asked.

"We'd have to siphon a lot of cars," Luke said. "Too many."

"Then we shall have to do it the old-fashioned way, sir. We have to go to the widow's walk." T.L. said.

No one moved for a moment, so he turned to Luke. "You'll need to transport us, sir."

CHAPTER 38

The Widow's Walk...

We transported as a group to the Pelican's widow's walk. T.L. brought a metal chair with him. The storm was raging, and lightning strikes were happening all up and down Virginia Dare Trail.

T.L. leaned over the railing and shouted, "There."

He put the chair in the middle of the deck. "Sir, you will sit here. Everyone, take off your shoes."

We all tossed our shoes to one side, and I sat on the chair. Next, T.L. physically moved Maggie and Elise so that Maggie was next to me and Elise was on her other side. Pulling Luke over to the railing, he left a small spot open between Luke and Elise.

"Everyone hold your hands out, palms up."

We all looked at each other and wondered what he was up to. One by one, we saw that our palms were wet. Every person in the line was going to act as a conduit.

T.L. is a genius.

Next, T.L. walked the line and checked each palm. "Maggie, take Jordan's hand. Make sure your wet palms press tightly against each other. Elise, you do the same with Maggie's other hand."

The storm moved closer to the Pelican. Lightning was now striking every few seconds, as the storm neared its peak. By the time it got to us, it would be at full strength.

T.L. shouted to Luke, "Hold your free hand out toward the beach and see if you can act as a lightning rod. I'll take your other hand." Once T.L. was connected to Luke, he watched the storm approach. When it was nearly overhead the Pelican, T.L. grabbed Elise's hand, wet palm to wet palm.

"Whatever you do, don't break the connection," T.L. shouted to us all. A mere instant later, Luke stretched his hand out toward a nearby lightning strike. It wasn't close enough, so Luke put one leg over the railing so he could extend his arm farther. Still not enough reach. He turned to us.

"Don't let go. None of you let go," Luke shouted.

Then Luke levitated, T.L. followed suit, as did Elise. Maggie's feet remained on the deck. This time, Luke was able to catch one of the off-shoots of lightning. I imagine we looked like the tail of one of those beautiful hang gliding kites they fly at Jockey's Ridge State Park.

I watched the electricity shoot through Luke's body from one arm straight through into T.L., and on to Elise and Maggie. Their hair stood on end, and their eyes were bright, shiny globes. It hadn't reached me yet, but I could smell their burning clothes and singed hair.

Criminy what was it going to do to me?

POW! The juice entered my arm first. Then it surged through my body. I looked at my feet. My toenails glowed. The hairs on my legs and arms ignited.

From start to finish, mere seconds passed, but it seemed like an eternity. I was the one to break the connection when I collapsed onto the deck floor. Everyone else tumbled to the deck next to me.

Perfect, now we are all dying.

I wasn't able to move my body, but I managed to turn my head to one side. I could see just enough to make out that Maggie and Elise were paler than usual. Black smudge marks spotted their necks. T.L.'s face was turned away from me, but I could see his hair was still smoldering. And Luke was nowhere to be seen.

Were we all shadow people now? Doomed to exist in the dark corners for eternity?

I passed out.

CHAPTER 39

The Aftermath...

When I came to, the storm had passed. I was alone on the widow's walk. Feeling like a sledgehammer had broken every bone in my body, I stumbled to my feet and shook off the cobwebs. It was several minutes before I noticed that the pain had evaporated. In fact, I felt alive and vibrant again.

It worked. Holy moly, if it didn't work.

I snapped my fingers and transported myself to the room where I usually met with Maggie and Elise. I found them, sitting at a card table, playing Old Maid with Luke. They were a somber group. As one unit, they turned to look in my direction.

"Are you guys okay?"

Maggie and Elise scampered over and examined every inch of me. Once they were satisfied I was okay, they kissed me on my cheeks, one on each side.

"We were so worried. You looked dead, I mean…dead." Elise blurted out. "But Luke said we have to give the process time before… you know."

"Do you have all your fingers and toes?" Maggie asked.

"I'm not a newborn. Of course, I have all my parts. In fact, I feel great."

Luke came to me and stared into my eyes for several moments before taking a step back. "It was a success."

"Where's T.L.? He didn't… he's not a shadow person now, is he?"

Please, please let him be okay.

"Some of his hair burned off. He's trying to rearrange the rest so you won't notice," Maggie said. She and Elise giggled behind their hands. It made me wonder if they were drunk on electric juice.

"But he's okay other than a few strands of singed hair?"

"Everyone is fine. But I can't say why because we should all be shadow people after doing such a crazy, irresponsible thing. We will not be doing anything like it again. Got it?" Luke demanded.

I had never seen Luke so upset before. But he was right.

"And you… you better wait and make sure you aren't going to burst into a shower of ash. That would be the last thing your Emily needs to see. We'll wait to make sure you have no side effects before you go to meet her."

A part of me had to agree with Luke, but I felt like Superman at the moment so it was all I could do not to zap over to Emily's right that moment.

The girls convinced me we could pass the time playing cards. Those girls sure were obsessed with their card games. But I guess they knew a thing or two about patience since they had been waiting centuries for their men to come home.

Eventually, T.L. came back, and we convinced him to play a few hands of cards. He had seen us playing Go Fish before and requested we play it with him. Luke wouldn't play for a few hands, he was still furious we had been so foolish. But eventually, he sat in his chair, and we played cards until it was almost time.

CHAPTER 40

Sometime in the late afternoon, it was time for me to prepare for my evening with Emily. Luke and I did a run through of sorts, and everything was fine. He lectured me on the reasons for setting a time limit on my stay and then handed me a beautifully crafted pendant on a silver chain.

"It's from all of us… even T.L. put in money. As it turns out, the girls and T.L. find lost money all the time." I must have given him an impatient look because he hurried on. "anyway, as a group we voted that you should give Emily a gift to memorialize your last night. Look on the back."

I turned the pendant over and saw it was engraved with my likeness and the words 'Forever Yours.'

"Who engraved it?"

"I did. Don't look at me like you're shocked or anything. I used to make my own comic books before my accident."

I grabbed Luke and gave him the hug I had learned to appreciate. I had become a hugger and I was happy he hugged me back.

"You better get over to Emily's. Right about now, Allie's telling her about your arrangement."

I shared a final look with Luke, grinned and snapped my fingers.

CHAPTER 41

As it turned out, I landed in Emily's living room, dab smack in front of her television. I had materialized in all my glory, full-bodied and exposed for everyone to see. And there was mood lighting. Emily didn't have electricity either. She had lit candles everywhere. Guess the storm had some side benefits for me.

A quick glance around the room told me that Allie was sitting in a chair, and Emily was on the couch, her legs tucked under her. Allie turned, looked at me and grinned so widely I thought I could hear her cheekbones crackling. Emily was another story.

Em turned her eyes toward me. They were as wide and as blue as they could be. Her lips were trembling. Em tried to stand, but she was shaking so much she fell back onto the couch. I walked over to her and knelt at her feet.

"I've missed you," I said in as calm a voice as I could muster. Luke and I never could figure out how to make me sound like I did when I was alive. My voice still screeched like an old radio that needed tuning. But I don't think that mattered to Em. She burst into tears and threw her arms around my neck. She squeezed so hard that I thought for a moment my head might pop off. Then she pulled back, looked me in the eye and rained kisses all over my face, wetting me with her tears.

Allie came over and put her hand on my shoulder.

"I am so glad you could come, Jordan. I'm going to go to my Pop's house for the night, so I'll say my goodbyes now. I hope one day I meet a man who will love me as much as you love Emily."

Allie kissed me on my head and walked out the door. But I barely noticed. I was drowning myself in Emily's eyes.

"How?" Emily asked me with her hands on both sides of my face.

"I can't explain it."

Emily grabbed my hands. "I won't let you leave me again."

I sat on the couch and pulled her onto my lap.

"Sweetheart, I'm not... Listen, I want us to enjoy this last night together. Let's not waste it on things we can't change."

Emily sighed and leaned against my chest. "But you feel so real."

The irony forced me to laugh. "Considering I'm dead, that's an interesting compliment."

Emily gazed at me with one eyebrow raised. "Well, I can see your sense of humor hasn't changed."

"Oh, before I forget, I have a present for you." I pulled the pendant necklace from my pocket. "Let me put it on you."

After I secured the clasp, Emily skipped over to the hall mirror to see how she looked in it. She held a candle up to get a better look.

"I love it," she whispered.

I walked over and stood behind her. Rubbing her shoulders, I gazed at her face in the mirror. She glowed.

When I turned the pendant over so she could see the etching on the back, Emily gasped. Her hands shook as she ran a fingertip over it.

"A last gift?" Emily swallowed her tears, trying her best to look brave. I knew her well enough that I could tell what she was thinking. At that moment, Emily was determined to not spend our last night crying. To tell you the truth, that tiny thing almost made me cry myself.

"I have to tell the truth. My new friends got it for me to give to you." Emily's frown and tilt of her head reminded me that she knew nothing about Luke and the others. She and I had been inseparable since the third grade, so we had always known the same people and we seldom kept secrets from one another. My other life was foreign to her, just as everything that had happened to her since the accident was foreign to me. She probably had new friends I'd never meet. New experiences I'd never share.

So I spend the next half hour telling her about my new life and some adventures I had experienced since death had knocked at my door. By the time I was finished, Emily seemed satisfied.

"I had envisioned you hanging out in a misty gray field somewhere. Not doing anything but waiting."

"Luke says I have choices right now. I can do something to help people while I wait for your time to come. I know it sounds morbid… me waiting for you to die. But…" I lifted her chin with my crooked finger and gazed into her mesmerizing eyes. "I promise you I will be there when it is your time to cross over. And in the meantime, since I can't be with you or be a doctor, I will be useful in a different way."

"Then this is our last night together? For real?"

I hung my head. I didn't want to make her cry, but I couldn't come up with anything to make the situation sound better.

Em lifted my head and kissed me on the lips as if it were our first kiss all over again. I was in the sixth grade again and over the moon. Of course, I responded. A little too anxiously I'm afraid. I pulled back to allow myself to calm down and noticed that Emily was wearing this crooked smile that she had whenever she was in charge in our romantic trysts. She ripped my shirt off. The buttons went flying.

"I'm a dirty girl. Are you dirty?"

I nodded my head like a bobble head doll on crack.

"I've got some new candles in the bathroom and some nice bath wash to try out."

I bent over and sniffed her top.

"You do smell a little ripe."

Emily gasped and gave me a playful shove as she scampered away from me. At the archway leading to the bedroom, she turned and gave me a come-hither look. Peeling off her shirt, Emily teased me with her zipper in her shorts, unzipping them slowly. Then she pushed them past her thighs and calves. Beckoning me with a crooked finger, she disappeared down the hall.

I didn't have to be asked twice. I rushed after Emily, stripping off the rest of my clothes as I made my way back to her shower.

I entered the bathroom just as Emily was lighting the candles she had mentioned. She list the last one and sashayed up to me as I stood frozen in the doorway, unable to take my eyes off of her. She took my hands and intertwined our fingers. That small movement took my breath and reserve away. With one swift motion, I lifted her onto the vanity and devoured her lips with mine.

Emily returned the favor by kissing and licking my chest as I twisted my fingers in the curls of her hair. I knew I needed to say something now before it was too late. I was torn because I didn't want to possibly mar the rest of the night, but I wanted to… no, I needed to say it.

"Em, later tonight when you go to sleep, I'm going to leave."

Em put her fingers in her ears so she wouldn't have to hear what I was about to say. Gently I took her hands with my own and held them as I continued.

"Please, hear me out. I will love you until the end of time, but you have to promise me you'll go on with your life. I want you to date… and fall in love… and get married again and have children. I'll be waiting for you when it's your time, and we'll go… into the light together, I promise. But Em, you deserve to be more than a lonely widow. Promise me you'll do all the things we didn't get to do."

Emily bit her lip. I could see she was fighting back the tears.

"I'll take a nod as a promise."

She nodded. Reluctantly, but she did.

"Shoot, we'll even take your husband with us if it's his time too."

Em giggled and said, "You will, huh?"

"Yes, I will. I think things are different in Heaven anyway. And if it's okay with you, I will pop in from time to time to see how you are doing. When I do, I'll leave you a shiny penny or a tiny trinket to let you know I was there. Would you be cool with that?"

"Yes," Emily whispered.

"Well, then… come here, stinky girl. Let's get you clean."

I pulled Emily against me and lifted her off the vanity as she wrapped her legs around my waist and leaned in.

Murmuring against my chest, she said, "I will always, forever and more, love you. I'll do as you ask. I'll date, I may even get married, but you will always be in my heart."

I carried Em into the shower. There we spent the next hour sudsing each other and kissing every inch of each other's body. And when we couldn't take any more, we toweled each other off and tumbled into her bed.

We made love as if it were our last time and of course, it was. I think I can safely say neither of us could get enough of the other.

Oh did you think I was going to share all the details? I did say I was one of the good guys, right? Well, good guys don't kiss and tell.

***

A couple of hours later, Emily fell asleep. She swore she wouldn't, but she did. I was okay with her sleeping since I never could say goodbye. Besides, I had to be on my way before I ran out of energy. I hoped it would be easier to leave this way, but it wasn't.

Lying beside her, I memorized every inch of her face, her body, her hair, her everything. And then I memorized them once more.

To be honest, I was supposed to be long gone by now, but I figured a few minutes wouldn't do any harm.

A few more minutes, I thought. *Two, maybe three.*

I inhaled the fragrance of Emily's hair and allowed myself to touch the curve of her hips a last time. Giving her a final kiss as she slept, I took a few steps toward the door.

I knew right away that something was wrong. My legs weren't working like normal. I looked down and saw my fog feet had returned. And I was fading. My energy was near depleted.

I prayed I could at least make it outside Emily's house. It took every bit of energy I could squeeze out, but I made it out the deck door and no further. I collapsed on the deck.

Something buzzed around my ears. I try to swat at the bug or whatever it was, but I had no energy left by then. I couldn't lift a finger.

Is it possible I am dying again?

My last effort was to try to send a telepathic message to Luke to say goodbye.

CHAPTER 42

The Waiting Game...

T.L. Daniels stood at the window, peering out at the street below. Worry crinkled his brow, and his hands gripped the window sill. He pushed away from the window and turned with a fury.

"Sir, the man has been gone too long."

Luke looked up from his cards and glanced at the window. Maggie and Elisc turned as well, they whispered to each other behind their hands. Glancing at the ladies, Luke got up and joined T.L. at the window.

"You are upsetting Maggie and Elise. Come on, T.L. play cards with us. If he's not back in an hour, we'll go look for him." Luke gave a nod to the others.

"Very well, sir. But one hour. No longer." T.L. insisted.

Luke pulled T.L. from the window and led him to the table. "Watch out for Maggie, I do believe she is a card shark."

Maggie laughed and lightly slapped Luke's hand. T.L. snorted.

"You know you are kinda cute when you are not so grumpy," Elise said and then immediately covered her mouth with her hands when she realized she had spoken out loud.

Luke and Maggie laughed. T.L. rolled his eyes and sat down.

"I thought we were going to play cards," T.L. grumbled.

Maggie sat down and began to deal the cards.

Luke swatted at his ear. Then he swatted again.

Maggie touched his arm, "Edna Jean is probably worried about Jordan."

Luke frowned. Shadow people steered clear of him for the most part. He wondered…

"I'm sorry Jordan is dead, but I'm happy I know him," Maggie commented.

"Yes, he is a fair man who cares about others," T.L. added as he examined his cards.

Surprised, Luke stared at T.L.

Maggie and Elise piped up, "Yes."

Luke reached to take a card from the pile. Suddenly, Elise shrieked and pointed to the window. Maggie turned to look as T.L. and Luke jumped to their feet.

There on the window were what looked to be hundreds of fireflies.

Stepping closer, Luke saw that they weren't bugs at all. They were shadow people in tiny forms. As he watched, they formed words on the window.

There was an 'h,' followed by an 'e' and an 'l.'

Maggie cried, "Help. Jordan needs help."

T.L. grabbed Luke's arm and turned him around. "Sir, we need to go to him. Now!"

"Hang on, T.L., you're going with me."

Luke put his hand on T.L.'s shoulder and snap! They were off to rescue Jordan.

CHAPTER 43

Jordan...

I came to in one of our charging houses with T.L. and Luke hovering over me. Their faces were scrunched with concern and worry. T.L. especially had anxiety written all over his body. At least, I thought the figure was T.L. I squinted my eyes and looked at him again. Sure enough, it was him, in a bright orange Hawaiian shirt and surfer shorts with his bulky boots.

I pulled off the mask they had duct taped over my face to feed me electricity.

"You stopped to take him shopping?" I barely got out before I had to put the mask back on my face and take in more electricity.

"Well, the dude deserved to look presentable, didn't he?' Luke laughed and slapped T.L. on his back. "We still have to find some sandals for him though. He looks almost like a model, doesn't he?"

When T.L. smoothed at his shirt with pride, even I had to smile. I tried to rise, but both men pushed me back on the bed.

"You need to rest. You damn near turned into one of the shadow people, sir." T.L. was insistent.

As I laid back and sucked on a little more electricity, I looked at the contraption they had jerry-rigged. It looked like a metal strainer with a series of long metal wires duct taped to it. The wires, in turn, were duct taped to the wall outlet. Not a pretty sight by any means but it did the trick. I looked at Luke and pointed to the outlet.

"T.L.'s idea. Turns out he was not exaggerating. He reads everything. I guess when you have nothing else to do, books fill your time. Turns out he likes books on electricity. And Frankenstein. The dude has a serious hard-on for monster books. If it weren't for him, we would have lost you to the shadow world."

After T.L. took a little bow, he wandered off. Luke came and sat on the edge of my bed.

"He's exploring. He knows he has to go back to the Pelican and his existence there, but while T.L. is out, he's making the most of his time. How do you feel?"

"Not bad. I could be better but considering everything, I'm not complaining."

"Good, after you get enough of a power boost, I'll take you to the Pelican to recuperate. The ladies are anxiously awaiting you. I do believe they will be spoiling you."

Luke moved to stand, I grabbed his arm to stop him.

"I want you to know how much I appreciate your help. I couldn't have done any of this without you or the others. I'm grateful for all of you."

Luke slipped a sincere smile on his face. I had never seen that before. Cocky? Yes. Smirky? Yes. Sincere? Not even close.

"I think we owe you more. You helped every single one of us. We had become complacent and satisfied with our existence. Now we all have hope again. The ladies and T.L. may be tethered to The Black Pelican, but now they know they can enjoy new pleasures again. By the way, you should thank Edna Jean when you see her."

"Edna Jean?"

"Apparently, the shadow people have a communication network of sorts. She had her people keeping an eye on you. When they saw you collapse, they got a message to me and the others. That's how we knew to come and rescue you."

I laid back and thought for a few seconds.

Wow… dead friends aren't all that different from live ones. Who would have thought?

"I'm guessing power's back on in the OBX?"

"I took a ride up and down Virginia Dare Trail while you were out. Most everyone has power now. I'm not sure about Ocracoke and some of the other places. But things are getting back to normal around here."

"By any chance…"

"Did I look in on Emily? Yes. I knew you'd ask. She's fine. Her parents are there now. At least I assume they are her parents. Very bossy people." Luke gave one of those 'wow' looks. I knew exactly what he was thinking.

"That's them."

"Anyway, Emily looks different. She looks as if she has accepted where she is in life. A lot like you look right now."

I nodded my head.

"I also have renewed excitement about my assignment here," Luke said.

"Your assignment?"

Luke nodded. "We're going talk more about that when you are better. I also want to talk to you about your purpose. I know what it is."

A loud crash grabbed our attention.

"T.L.," we yelled in unison.

CHAPTER 44

A few months later, I was happy to leave The Black Pelican. While I enjoyed the company of the ladies and T.L., I needed to get out in the world again. I was embracing my dead self and was ready to find out what my purpose in the Living Dead world would be.

I immediately headed to the Dune Burger. As I suspected, Luke was there, people watching and catching rays. I walked over and grabbed a chair.

"Good day for surfing."

"Yup," Luke said, not moving a muscle to get up. After a few seconds, I got the hint.

"So we're going to chill for a while." I leaned back and raised my face to catch some rays.

"Yup. I plan to spend some time appreciating the beauty of humanity."

Luke pointed to a young couple teaching their little boy to ride a bike. We enjoyed watching them until they disappeared around the bend.

Then a teenaged couple came along arguing as they walked along the beach road. Both had plenty to say to the other, but it looked like the couple did so respectfully. At one point, the teenagers stopped walking and stared at each other. I was sure the fight was about to escalate, but the boy put his arms around the girl and hugged her. End of argument. They went back walking again, hand in hand, arms swinging. All was good in their world once again.

"The first afternoon we met," Luke blurted out.

"I remember it."

"It wasn't an accidental meeting."

"I know." My voice sounded like I wanted to say more and I did but I wasn't sure how accepting Luke would be. So I tried to choose my words carefully. Before I could finish my thought, Luke beat me to it.

"What is it you want to say, Doc?"

"I have an idea for helping the shadow people."

"I figured that's how you'd been spending your time. Hit me with it."

"What if we juice them up again? Except in tiny spurts. We could build up their capacities again over time. I've been working with T.L. on a way to do that."

Luke laughed so hard that he fell out of his chair. He said, "I'm not laughing at you. It's just the thought of working with T.L. is quite a visual in my mind."

"He's a smart guy. I told you he was falsely accused."

"I agree, but he's still… crabby. So what did he come up with?" Luke stood up and turned to me.

"It's sort of an electronic eyedropper that measures out exact amounts of electricity. If we get the doses right, the shadow people will eventually become like the other ghosts. At least then, they have something to look forward to." I jumped up, excited at the prospect of helping Edna Jean.

"Sounds like it just might work. Do you remember the first time I called you Doc, and you thought you weren't a doctor anymore?" Luke asked as he moved next to me.

I suddenly felt melancholy thinking about my lost career.

"You will always be a healer," Luke said as he touched my chest. "You were born a healer. And now is a perfect time to bring up a new twist."

"Let me guess… you're not a ghost."

"Oh I am, but I am also a transition angel. Everything I told you was true. I died and became a ghost like you, but one day I was awarded the status of transition angel. You see, that's where my dead talent lies. I'm good at helping souls find their way, whether it's to adjust to their new existence or to enter the light and go to Heaven."

"So why can't you help me go to Heaven?" I asked.

"It's a bit complicated. After the accident, do you remember seeing a bright light?"

"I don't recall any lights. I only remember Emily needed my help."

"There was a light. It was God calling you to Heaven. You ignored it to help Emily."

My mind flew back to that night. In a series of flashbacks, I recalled all that had happened. Sure enough, there was a light.

"You're right... all this time and I just didn't remember it."

"There's a reason for that. You didn't go into the light because it wasn't your time. There are many people you need to help before you are ready to let go of your existence here. People like Edna and her shadow friends, T.L. with his anger, and the girls who existed merely to wait until you came along. Even George who needed a friend. And there will be other people who need your help... in case you think you are done."

"I didn't do anything special. I only did what any other decent person would do."

"I don't believe any of your friends would agree with you. You are a caring man willing to sacrifice yourself for others. That, Doc, makes you special. And that is why I knew you had to become my protégé. And now you are going to be my army of one. Together, we will help people transition. And for many of them, we will help them go into the light."

"Can I go with Emily? Can I walk with her into the light when her time comes?" It was important to me to hear him say yes. I wasn't disappointed.

"In a short answer, yes. But there may be complications."

"Don't tell me any more right now. I'll deal with it later. So what's next for me?"

"Well, Dude, since you are my army of one, I am authorized to make you my assistant transition angel."

"George thought I was an angel the first night I met him."
Luke smiled.

"He could see your halo even then. You see, Doc? Destiny."

"Me. An angel. Wow."

"So, later, tonight, there is a little girl in Duck who is going to drown. She's going to have a tough time and need some gentle assistance to adjust. We'll have to dress up for this one. So... how do you feel about being a princess or Pretty Pony?"

Luke now had his eye on a pretty girl walking a tiny dog who imagined he was a lot bigger than the size of his body.

"Can't we save her?"

"Unfortunately, we are not allowed to change the future or the past. All we can do is comfort the little girl and help her to adjust."

"So she'll be going into the light."

"Not yet. The child doesn't believe in God right now. She'll transition to her new existence here, and later after she comes to believe, we will show her the light."

"Wait a minute… is that where you've been disappearing to? Helping the newly dead transition?"

"Yup." Luke grabbed his surfboard. "Surf's up, Dude."

***

Luke and I surfed most of the afternoon while we waited until it was time for us to go to Duck. Eventually, we paddled out to a calm area and laid on our backs on our surfboards, enjoying the afternoon. It gave me time to reflect on my new assignment.

I also decided to that it was okay to allow myself to count the days until I could drop in on Emily for a brief look-see. I made a commitment to myself that I wouldn't do it more than once a month and less than that once she started dating. And I made a mental note to find some pretty stones and shiny pennies first. Promises must be kept, after all.

I also made a note to find some special gifts to give the girls for taking care of me, and something for T.L. A new Hawaiian shirt, the orange one was getting kinda rank. And something for Luke. A new skateboard. Yeah.

You know what? Being dead really isn't all that bad when you've got a few good friends.

THE END

ABOUT THE AUTHOR

Suzi Albracht and her boyfriend, Tim, live near Annapolis, Maryland. She enjoys writing stories that have characters with intense interpersonal relationships. When she is not writing, she is shooting pool or taking long country rides in Tim's 70 Camaro.

Suzi has these books on Amazon in addition to this one.
The Siren of Diamond Shoals
Death Most Wicked
The Devil's Lieutenant
Scorn Kills.

You can contact Suzi on Twitter by her handle @SuziAlbracht.

Look for the other titles by Suzi on Amazon.com.

Made in the USA
Middletown, DE
09 August 2019